HOPS FOR THE HOLIDAYS

A HOLIDAY NOVELLA

SPIRIT OF HOPS
BOOK THREE

J. E. JOYCE

Hops for the Holidays

SPIRIT OF HOPS SERIES · BOOK THREE

J. E. JOYCE

To my brewery boys ~
One time just wasn't enough... Thank you for being such amazing
sports and humoring this crazy author and her bonkers ideas.

and this is still all you're fault and only have yourselves to blame.

Callum's life is full to the brim—building a career he loves with Spirit of Hops Brewstillery, raising his vivacious six-year-old daughter, Georgie, and building a life with his boyfriend, Charlie, the brewery's charming and endlessly patient bar manager. With Christmas approaching, the trio is settling into their rhythm as a family, navigating the chaos and magic of the holiday season together.

Between Georgie's excitement over baking cookies with Charlie's big-hearted family and the quiet moments shared beneath the glow of Christmas lights, Callum can't help but feel like he's finally found the life he's always wanted. But as New Year's Eve approaches, Charlie has a plan to take their love story to the next level—a surprise that could change everything for the better.

This heartwarming, steamy, holiday romance is a celebration of love, laughter, and the joy of building a family together.

Perfect for fans of small-town charm, found family, and happily-ever-afters, *Hops for the Holidays* is brimming

with warmth and romance, leaving you smiling long after
the last page.

CHAPTER ONE

CHARLIE

DECEMBER 4TH

Spirit of Hops Brewstillery smells like hops and burnt pretzels. Again.

I know my man has a brilliant idea he swears is going to turn out amazing and be a bestseller when it's done, but dear lord, I'm over the brew-day-stink from the special secret recipe he's using to create the toasted marshmallow, whatever it is he's brewing. He won't give me details because he is under the impression I can't keep a secret. No idea where he got that from. No idea whatsoever.

Ya tell a regular about the new position your boyfriend taught you the night before that literally blew your goddamn mind *once*, and suddenly you can't be trusted with secrets. What's this world coming to?

"Hey, Charlie, I'm gonna need a hand," Callum calls from the back, his voice muffled by the clutter of kegs and equipment.

With a grin, I slide the last clean glass into the rack and

glance toward the gap behind the bar that leads to the brewing equipment in the back, mostly hidden from customer view. "What kind of hand?" I call as I wave to Emily, who's behind the bar with me, signaling she'll be on her own for a bit. "Labor-type hand? Emotional Support hand? My-right-hand-is-busy-so-use-my-left kind of hand?"

Callum pokes his head out, his sandy brown hair dusted with what I hope is dust or flour, for some reason, and not some horrifying yeast experiment gone wrong. His cheeks are flushed, and his expression says *you're the love of my life, but also a giant pain in my ass...* in more ways than one, thank you very much. I open my mouth to remind him of that fact, but he cuts me off before I can.

"Kegs jammed," he says flatly, jerking a thumb behind him. "And unless you want me to introduce IPA Fridays with a nice metallic undertone particularly enticing to vampires, you might want to get back there and help me."

"On it," I reply, wiping my hands on the bar rag that lives in my back pocket when working as I round the corner. "But just for the record, *Metallic Undertone* would be a kickass band name."

The look Cal sends me says he's weighing the pros and cons of putting me inside the keg instead of fixing it.

The brewing area is a maze of stainless steel tanks, hoses, and that one terrifying cleaning robot that Mac insists is "completely safe" but looks like it's two bolts away from a Terminator reboot. I follow Cal through the heavy steel door behind the massive industrial cooler and find the offending keg sitting lopsided under the tap line. Callum immediately crouches beside it, muttering to himself like I assume he's been doing for at least the last twenty minutes before mustering the will to ask me for help. I may adore the man, but he has a stubborn streak a mile wide.

"Looks like you've got it handled," I say, leaning casually against a stack of pony kegs inside the door. "Good talk."

"Charlie," he warns, his voice low and dangerous in that *my child is scarier than you. This isn't my first rodeo* kind of way. Why the hell is that so hot?

"Fine, fine," I say, crouching beside him. "But if I break a nail, you're paying for the manicure."

Callum shoots a pointed look at my work-rough hands and clean but short nails before rolling his eyes, doing his best to hide a smile. "Just hold it steady."

We work in silence for a minute, the kind of silence that feels like a conversation when you've been together long enough. It's only been a few months, but something about Callum feels like I've known him forever. Maybe it's the way he snorts when I tell a dumb joke, or it could be the way his face softens every time Georgie walks into the room.

Georgie, his six-year-old daughter, is a certified menace. Also, she's perfect. I'd die for her, but I'd probably complain about it the whole time while she heckled me from the side-lines. It's how we show our love.

"Almost there," Callum grunts, tugging on the stubborn keg. His muscles flex under his Spirit of Hops branded T-shirt, and I absolutely don't stare. Okay, I stare a little, but I definitely don't drool. Not at all.

"There," he says, sitting back on his heels as the line clicks back into place. He grins triumphantly, and I swear he gets hotter every time he fixes something or smiles at me like that. "Crisis averted."

"Beer drinkers everywhere thank you for your service," I say, clapping him on the shoulder. "Now, let's get out of here before that cleaning robot stops playing nice and takes over."

We head back to the bar, where a small crowd has started to gather. I slip back into bartender mode while Callum ducks out to pick Georgie up from school. I quickly lose track of time and lose myself in my favorite part of my job. What keeps me coming back is chatting with the regulars and enjoying the community we've built around Spirit of Hops over the years.

Somehow, I get pulled into a discussion about cars with a couple of the regulars, which inevitably leads to me getting trolled for the rusted heap of steel I call my truck.

"That thing still runs?" Fran calls from her usual spot at the far end of the bar. Her glass is already half-empty— impressive, considering she just sat down ten minutes ago. "What happened to that new one you were drooling over last summer?"

"Turns out they don't take beer as payment," I deadpan, grabbing the IPA she's working through and topping it off. I slide it back to her with a grin.

As she snorts into her beer, I glance at the clock on the wall — 3:45pm, which means I have about fifteen minutes before Callum and Georgie show up for our daily after-school hang-out ritual. Well, it's not so much a ritual as a sneaky way for me to get in good with a six-year-old who's probably smarter than I was at twice her age and with triple the attitude.

The door swings open a little while later, and the chilly December air blasts through the taproom like it owns the place. I look up from polishing a glass to see the man himself walk in. Callum Bowers, brewer, king of my damn heart, and the only person I've ever seen make steel-toed boots look sexy. He strides in with that confident air that drew me in from the first moment I saw him, with Georgie skipping beside him, her pink coat flapping like a superhero's cape.

"Afternoon, boss," Callum says, sliding behind the bar like he's clocking back in. His lips curl into that small, soft smile that always makes stomach flip and my heart skip.

"Not your shift," I say, setting the glass down before

leaning in to give him a quick kiss on his scruffy cheek. "And if you're here to mooch free beer, you've gotta at least pretend to be charming first."

"Pretend?" His eyebrow arches. "I'm pretty sure I charmed you without even trying."

He's got me there, but I'm not giving him the satisfaction. "That's bold talk from a man who tripped over a keg in front of an entire bachelorette party last week."

Georgie bursts into giggles. "You fell down, Daddy?"

Callum groans, rubbing the back of his neck. "It was one time."

"Legendary," I add, leaning on the bar with a shit-eating grin. "I'm sure Kendric has security footage somewhere. I might convince him to break it out for Christmas cards this year."

Callum flips me off, but his grin takes all the bite out of it.

Georgie climbs onto a barstool, plopping her sparkly unicorn backpack onto the bar top. "Charles, do you have cookies?" she asks in the overly formal, borderline British accent she uses when trying to be polite and proper. It's legitimately the most adorable thing I have ever heard in my damn life.

"Do I have cookies?" I repeat, pretending to be horrified. "George! You wound me. Of course I have cookies." I grab a small plate from under the counter and pull out a stack of sugar cookies my mom dropped off earlier, just for her. Georgie's eyes light up as I slide the plate over to her.

"Score!" she squeals, snatching one off the top of the stack. Callum clears his throat before she can get the cookie to her mouth, drawing both our attentions.

"Georgie," he says in that dad tone that means business. "What do we say when someone gives us something nice?"

Georgie looks at him, then back at me. "Charles, will you marry me?"

I can't contain my choked snort of surprise as the taproom around us erupts into laughter, and Callum pinches the bridge of his nose. "That's not—never mind."

"You're welcome for the cookies, George. And pretty sure your dad has a rule about not getting married until you are at least 45, so let's wait on that one, k?" I say, trying to hold back my laughter, desperate to not hurt her feelings or make this sweet little girl think she said something wrong. She considers my response for a moment before a bright smile breaks across her angelic little face.

"Thanks, Charles. You're the best!" she replies.

"Don't let your dad hear you say that," I whisper conspiratorially, earning another round of giggles.

Callum watches us with a warm expression that makes my insides do weird, fluttery things I never would have thought I could feel before he crashed into my life. Or I guess technically, I crashed into his, but that's ancient history now, right?

I straighten and clear my throat. "So," I say, going back to polishing glasses that absolutely don't need it, but I need the distraction because if I look at him too long, I might do something embarrassing like sigh dreamily. "What's the plan for you two troublemakers this afternoon?"

"Daddy said you could help me pick out a Christmas Present for Nana Barbie," Georgie chimes through a mouthful of cookies.

"Did he now?" I glance at Callum.

He shrugs. "You're the Larson Family expert. Who better to ask?"

"That's true; I have known her my whole life," I say, straightening up and shooting Georgie a wink, earning yet another crumb-filled giggle from her. "And lucky for you, Nana Barbie is easy to shop for. Jewelry, wine, or anything with a cat on it. Bonus points if it sparkles."

"Sparkly wine with cats?" Georgie asks, tilting her head like she's just discovered the secret of the universe.

"Exactly," I say with a grin. Callum just shakes his head, but his shoulders relax, and I know he's glad he came back today. He works hard—sometimes too hard—and getting him to unwind takes effort. Easing Georgie and making her happy is one of my favorite cures.

"So," I say, resting my elbows on the bar. "How's it feel being part of the crazy Larson Christmas circus this year?"

"Loud," he replies instantly, then smirks. "But good. Georgie's excited, which means I'm excited by default. And your mom already sent me three different green bean casserole recipes, so I think I'm officially in. Though Ollie cornered me the other day and demanded me pick milk or potatoes, I had zero idea what to say, so... there's that."

"It's a lefse thing. I'm sure you'll get a full rundown, and Ollie is a loon, so just ignore him," I say. "As for Nana Barbie, she loves a captive audience, and you made the mistake of mentioning that you have tried baking even once in your life. You're her new favorite since all of us heathen boys can't bake to save our lives. Sorry, George, but your dad is outshining us all."

"That's okay," Georgie says, licking cookie crumbs off her fingers. "I still get to help her bake, and Daddy says I'm the best cookie decorator in the whole world."

"She is," Callum confirms. "But we don't mention the unfortunate frosting incident with Betha."

Georgie gasps, whipping her head toward her father, sending her mop of blond ringlets swirling around her. "You promised not to tell!"

"I didn't say anything specific," he teases, reaching over and ruffling her curls.

Watching them together is one of my favorite things about this relationship. Callum is so patient and steady, balancing Georgie's endless energy with his quiet kind of joy that's ridiculously attractive. And I just love that I get to be even a small part of it.

Before I get too lost in the thought, the door swings open again, and Alfie, one of my brothers, steps in.

"Charlie," he calls, loud enough to startle half the bar. "You got that list mom is asking for, or am I gonna have to make a scene?"

I sigh. "You live to make scenes. Don't act like it's for my benefit."

"Fair point." He walks up to the bar, sending Callum a friendly chin lift and ruffling Georgie's curls. "Hey, man. Ready for the insanity this weekend?"

"Not even a little," Callum responds, deadpan.

"You'll survive," Alfie assures him. "Just don't drink anything Ollie gives you without checking the color first. That's how we lost Uncle Joe for like two hours last year."

Georgie's eyes go wide. "Did he get lost in the snow?"

"Worse," Alfie says gravely. "He got lost in the karaoke machine."

She gasps, and I shake my head. "Alfie, stop terrifying children."

He shrugs. "Just saying. Holiday dinner's a battlefield. You think Thanksgiving was bad? That was nothin' compared to what's coming," he responds ominously. The drama queen.

"Then it's a good thing Callum's a survivor," I say, tossing the man in question a wink.

Callum's gaze softens, and the rest of the world fades away for a second. I want to tell him I'll be there to survive anything with him, but it feels too big for this moment. So, instead, I give him a quiet smile, hoping he knows what I mean.

Alfie clears his throat dramatically. "Not to interrupt this Hallmark moment, but I still need that list, bro."

"I'll email it to her, like I told her the last three times she asked," I say, rolling my eyes. "Now leave before you corrupt any more six-year-olds."

He mock-salutes and heads out, an icy blast of air sweeping through the taproom in his wake.

Callum leans against the bar as Georgie returns to her cookies, his expression thoughtful. "Your family's... a lot."

"You think?" I grin. "You haven't even met Eddie yet. He's the wild card."

"I thought Alfie was the wild card... or Ollie..."

"Oh, no. Ollie's the chaotic baby of the family. Alfie's a loose cannon. Wild card and loose cannon are totally different things."

Callum chuckles, shaking his head. "And which one would that make you?"

"The stable one," I scoff at the dumb question.

"Right. Still, your family seems so solid. You all know your place and embody your strengths. I feel like I'm wading in the ocean every day, unable to quite reach shore." He pauses, looking down at the cracked and scoured bar top, lost in thought. "And yet, somehow, they all seem to like me."

I can't help but soften at his words. He thinks we have shit together? That's laughable. Still, we know who we are and don't water it down for anyone. But Callum? He's everything. I want to tell him I'll always be there, that I'll be his raft in that ocean he's fighting. I'll be the one there to keep his head above the waves. We'll reach the shore together... but this isn't the place, and I've always believed that actions speak louder than words.

"They don't like you," I say, leaning over to steal a quick kiss. "They love you. Big difference."

Georgie groans. "Ew. Kissing."

Without missing a beat, I pull back just enough to lick a long stripe up Callum's cheek, topping it off with a quick peck on the temple before turning a shit-eating grin on a now squealing and cackling Georgie.

The afternoon slips by with a rhythm I've grown to love: the clinking of glasses, the murmur of voices, and the easy presence of Callum and Georgie. I don't know what I did to get this lucky, but I'm holding onto it with both hands.

As I watch Georgie finish her cookies as Callum helps her with a homework worksheet, I feel a pang of something big and terrifying and wonderful.

This—us—isn't perfect. But it's ours. And I wouldn't trade it for anything.

CHAPTER TWO

CALLUM

DECEMBER 5TH

The release bell rings as Charlie and I pull up in the carpool lane in front of the school, and a hoard of children full of pent-up energy from their long day pour out of the building. Georgie is leading the charge, with backpack flapping, hair escaping from under her neon green hat that looks like a frog, and a wide grin that makes my heart squeeze. She spots us immediately and waves like she's directing traffic, somehow commandeering at least three other kids to wave along with her.

Charlie leans across the center console and squints through the windshield. "Are they doing a choreographed goodbye routine?"

"Possibly," I say. "Or she's recruiting for some kind of kid uprising. Hard to tell."

"I feel like we should be worried," Charlie says, head shaking with a laugh.

I sigh, unbuckling my seatbelt. "We should have been worried a long time ago. That ship's long since sailed."

As I step out of the car, Georgie bounces toward me, her frog hat askew and her unicorn backpack dangling precariously off one shoulder. "Daddy! Charles!"

"George!" Charlie answers, stepping out of the car and giving an exaggerated salute.

"Hey, slow down, kiddo!" I call, but it's too late—she barrels into me like a cannonball, nearly knocking me back a step.

"You're early!" she says breathlessly.

"I'm right on time," I correct, tugging one dangling end of her hat. "You're just fast."

"Like lightning," Charlie teases from where he leans against the passenger door of my car, arms crossed and smiling as he watches us. He's got this way of looking at Georgie that turns me into a puddle every time—like she's already family to him. Like he's all in.

"Did you leave any smarts in there today, or did you keep them all for yourself?" he asks, crouching down to her level and opening his arms for a hug.

Georgie's brow furrows in that comically serious way of hers before she steps into him for a brief but tight hug. "I think I kept most of them. But I shared some with Harper because she didn't know how to spell 'Tyrannosaurus.'"

Charlie whistles low. "Tyrannosaurus, huh? Someone's aiming for extra cookies at Nana Barbie's."

"Obviously," she grins, preening under the compliment, and I swear, this kid is going to have Charlie wrapped around her little finger in no time. Not that he's putting up much of a fight. As he straightens back to standing, Georgie reaches for his hand and mine as we walk around the car to her side to get her settled.

Charlie's been coming with me to pick her up more often

lately. Watching him with her—easy, natural, patient—it's like we've been a trio for years, not just a few months, and it makes my heart melt every time I see them together.

Once Georgie is buckled into her booster seat in the back —after an extended debate over whether she's tall enough to go without it (she's not)—we hit the road. Charlie takes over DJ duties, so the car is soon filled with a very eclectic mix of holiday songs and bad pop ballads.

"Is this Riah Carey?" Georgie asks, tilting her head like she's trying to decide if she approves.

"Absolutely," Charlie says. "A Christmas icon that gets brought out of cold storage once a year for the holidays. You're welcome."

I struggle to suppress a snort of laughter at his explanation, wishing I could smack him for it without getting yelled at by the tiny tyrant in the back.

Georgie shrugs, the movement catching my eye in the rearview mirror. "She's okay, I guess."

Charlie gasps, clutching his chest like she's mortally wounded him. "Okay? *Okay?!* She's a legend, George. A queen! You take that back!" he demands, hamming it up for her.

She giggles, clearly delighted by his dramatics. "Eh, still not as good as Elsa."

Charlie gives me a long-suffering look, and I smirk back at him. "Don't fight it. You'll never win against Frozen."

He mutters something about "kids these days," but he's smiling as he says it.

As we pull onto the main road through town, Georgie starts swinging her legs, the soles of her sparkly sneakers thumping softly against the seat. "Oh! Guess what?!" she asks, bouncing in her booster.

"What?" I ask, bracing myself. You never know with Georgie.

"My teacher said I'm good at *critical thinking* today!"

"Did she?" I glance at Charlie, who is desperately trying to suppress a laugh. "What exactly does that mean?"

"It means I asked a lot of questions today. Important questions."

Charlie grins. "Like what?"

Georgie's eyes light up as she nods emphatically. "Like, 'Why don't adults get recess?' and 'Why can't we have chocolate milk every day?' and 'Why are adults obsessed with socks?' They're no fun!"

"I see you're tackling the big issues," I say, doing my best to sound solemn while holding back a grin.

"It's important to ask questions," Georgie says, her tone very serious.

Charlie turns around in his seat, his dimpled smile directed at her. "It sure is. But did you get any answers?"

"Not really," she admits. "But I'm working on it."

Unable to let quiet reign for more than a moment or two, it's not long before Georgie starts down her next line of questioning. "So," she says. "Tell me more about your family, Charles."

"More? You've already met almost all of them and know they're crazy," Charlie answers, smirking my way.

"They're not crazy," Georgie argues. "They're fun."

"That's debatable."

"Don't listen to him, Georgie," I say, glancing at her in the mirror. "He's just bitter because they don't think he's the funniest Larson."

"They *know* I'm the funniest Larson," Charlie retorts, leaning back dramatically. "They're just jealous."

Georgie giggles. "What about your brothers? You have three, right?"

"Four," Charlie corrects, holding up fingers as he ticks them off. "Donnie, Alfie, Ollie, and Eddie. But

Eddie's off saving the world or some shi... stuff. Some stuff."

"Nice catch," I tease under my breath with a laugh.

"Yeah, nice catch," Georgie chimes.

"Vulcan hearing." I shake my head, trying not to laugh.

"The kid catches everything," Charlie sighs.

"Wait, you said saving the world?" she asks, wonder in her little voice.

"Yeah, I'm not 100% sure what he does exactly," Charlie explains. "But he's on assignment in some place so remote, even the bugs have passports."

Georgie's eyes widen. "Cool! I know Ollie is silly and has all those pretty tattoos that Daddy says I can't ask to color 'cause it's rude. And Alfie looks like one of the Vikings from How to Train Your Dragon and has a laugh that makes my ears hurt. But what about Donnie? He's only been at Nana Barbies once when I'm there. Is he nice?"

If those aren't the most accurate descriptions of his brothers, I don't know what are.

Charlie raises an eyebrow, glancing at me before answering. "Nice? I mean, yeah. Donnie's great. Quiet, though. Definitely not the life of the party."

"He's mysterious," I add.

"Broody," Charlie corrects.

"He's an artist. What do you expect?" I ask.

"Wears a lot of black when he's not covered in car grease or wearing his coveralls for work," Charlie continues, nodding solemnly.

Georgie's mouth falls open. "He sounds so cool! Does he have a girlfriend?"

Charlie sputters. "What? Why're you asking, George?"

"I'm just curious," she says innocently, but the glint in her eye says otherwise.

I choke on a laugh at the sheer bluntness of her question,

and Charlie chuckles, turning in his seat to face her. "Nope. Donnie's single."

Georgie taps her chin like she's mulling this over. "Maybe he needs to find someone special. Like how Daddy found you."

Charlie throws me a sly look, his eyebrows raised. "What do you think, Callum? Should we let Georgie play matchmaker?"

"Oh, absolutely not," I say, trying to keep a straight face. "I've seen what she does with her dolls. The last time Barbie went on a date, Ken ended up with a broken leg."

"Ken deserved it," Georgie says solemnly.

Charlie bursts out laughing, and I can't help but join in. This kid, I swear.

"Hmm," Georgie says, and I swear I can see the gears turning in her head.

"That's a dangerous sound," I mutter under my breath.

"What is?" she asks, all innocence.

"That little 'hmm' of yours. It's how all your plans start."

She grins but says nothing, which is even more concerning.

———

LATER THAT EVENING, after dinner and the requisite debate over whether bedtime is a "suggestion" (it is not), I'm folding laundry while Georgie flits around the living room, pretending her stuffed animals are having a snowball fight. She's in her element, fully committed to the chaos, when she suddenly stops and looks at me like she's had the greatest epiphany of her life.

"Daddy!"

"What's up, Trouble?" I ask, holding up one of her socks.

"Have you considered inventing socks that don't vanish in the dryer? It would save me a fortune."

She ignores the sock, marching up to me with the air of someone about to drop a bombshell. "See? Adults and socks! Anyway, don't distract me. I was gonna say, I know what I'm going to do for Christmas."

"Let me guess. Eat all the cookies and blame it on Charlie?"

"No!" She rolls her eyes, hands on her hips. "I'm going to find someone for Donnie!"

I blink at her. "What?"

"You heard me."

"Yeah, I heard you. I'm just trying to process the fact that you've decided to play Cupid for a fully grown, functional adult who has said absolutely nothing about wanting to find someone."

She flops onto the couch dramatically, crossing her arms. "You said I was a good matchmaker."

"When did I say that?"

"Remember when I made you and Charlie sit next to each other at movie night? That was me."

I laugh, sitting beside her. "Pretty sure Charlie and I didn't need your help."

"But it worked, didn't it?"

"Fair point."

She grins triumphantly, then leans forward, resting her chin on her hands. "Donnie needs someone nice. Someone who likes cookies and animals and isn't afraid of the dark."

"Why the dark?"

"Because mysterious people always like the dark."

"You're an expert on mysterious people now?"

"Yes."

I shake my head, chuckling. "Okay, Matchmaker McGee, what's your big plan?"

"I don't have all the details yet," she admits, her face scrunching up in thought. "But I know it's going to be perfect."

"Georgie…" I pause, choosing my words carefully. "It's really sweet that you want Donnie to be happy, but matchmaking isn't always easy. Sometimes, people have to figure things out on their own."

She frowns, clearly not a fan of this revelation. "But what if he doesn't figure it out?"

"Then it'll happen when it's meant to happen," I say, brushing a strand of hair from her face.

"Trust me, kiddo, love has a funny way of showing up when you least expect it."

"Like with you and Charlie?"

I smile. "Exactly."

She seems to consider this for a moment, then nods decisively. "Okay. But if Donnie looks sad at Christmas, I'm helping."

I laugh, pulling her into a hug. "Deal. But no matchmaking without permission."

"Fine," she says, though her tone suggests she's already found a loophole.

As I tuck her into bed later, I can't help but marvel at the way her little mind works. She's always been a force of nature—curious, determined, and too clever for her own good.

I kiss her forehead, pulling the blankets up to her chin. "Goodnight, kiddo. Sweet dreams."

"Goodnight, Daddy." She pauses, her eyes sparkling. "Do you think Donnie likes cookies?"

"Goodnight, Georgie," I say firmly, fighting a smile.

As I turn off the light and close the door, I can't help but shake my head. Charlie better warn his brother—because

Georgie's got her sights set on him, and there's no stopping her when she's on a mission. And if Donnie knew what was coming, he'd probably run for the hills.

CHAPTER THREE

CHARLIE

DECEMBER 7TH

Saturday mornings are sacred in my house. The coffee's always strong, the music's always playing, and the vibe is always chill. At least, that's how it usually is.

This Saturday, it's one of those idyllic, postcard-perfect moments that Hallmark would kill for—minus the slightly lopsided tree, the Muppet Christmas Carol playing on repeat in the background, and that I'm stuck untangling what must be the world's largest knot of Christmas lights. My tree is fake—don't judge me; it comes in three pre-lit pieces, but it still requires more lights because I'm extra like that.

"This is why I hate pre-lit trees… they lie. They *say* they come fully lit but clearly require just as many additional lights as any other. I mean, come on now. In what world is that enough lights?" I mutter, wrestling with the string of lights like it's a python.

"You're the one who insists on more lights. I would be

fine with just the ones already on there," Callum points out, perched on the couch's armrest like some smug Christmas elf. He's holding Georgie's latest masterpiece—a paper snowflake that somehow looks like a chicken. It's amazing.

"I stand by my decision," I say, glaring at the lights. "But these things? These are an affront to humanity. I swear they tangle themselves on purpose."

"They're conspiring against you," Callum agrees solemnly, his lips twitching.

"Exactly. Thank you for understanding," I say, shooting him a grin.

"Need some help, Charles?" Georgie asks, hopping down from her stool at the breakfast bar where she's been coloring ornaments she and Betha made from salt dough last week.

"Do I *need* help?" I repeat, glancing at her. "No. Will I *accept* help? Also no. This is personal now."

She giggles, hopping back onto the chair. "You're silly."

"Silly but determined," I say, finally freeing one loop of lights from the knot. "What about you, George? You're awfully quiet over there. Plotting something?"

"Noooo," she says, her voice an octave too high to be convincing. "I'm just making an ornament for Uncle Donnie."

Callum groans softly. "Here we go."

"What? He needs a Christmas present."

I shoot Callum a look, grinning. "Your daughter is unstoppable. You should be proud."

"I am. I just wish her determination didn't always involve meddling in other people's lives."

"She's a visionary," I say.

"She's a six-year-old," he counters with an eye-roll.

"Same thing."

Georgie doesn't even look up, fully immersed in her project. "It's a reindeer with sparkly antlers. He'll love it."

Callum leans back, pinching the bridge of his nose. "I'm in so much trouble."

It takes me another hour of fighting with the lights that I swear grow extra limbs and branches and damn tentacles just to fuck with me before I get everything untangled, and we are finally ready to put everything together. By the time I'm ready, I have a six-year-old tornado zooming through my living room, tangled in a strand of tinsel that's shedding glitter like it's her mission to single-handedly redecorate my hardwood floors.

"George, you're shedding," I smirk, leaning against the kitchen counter with my coffee mug.

"I'm not shedding," she says, twirling like a sugar-hyped ballerina. "I'm spreading cheer."

"Same thing."

"Daddy!" she yells over her shoulder. "Charlie's being a Grinch!"

"I heard," Callum calls back, appearing in the doorway with a box of ornaments. His lips twitch like he's torn between scolding me and laughing. "Charlie, play nice or no cookies for you."

"Don't threaten me with a bad time."

Georgie stops twirling long enough to plop onto the couch, a glittery, giggling mess. "What are we doing first? Lights or ornaments?"

"Lights," I answer, setting my mug down and clapping my hands. "Always the lights first. Ornaments come last because that's the grand finale. You don't eat dessert before dinner, do you?"

She considers this like it's the most profound thing she's ever heard. "What if you're having ice cream for dinner?"

"She's got you there," Callum says with a grin, carrying the ornament box to the tree.

"Don't encourage her," I mutter, grabbing another box of decorations.

Once the lights are finally on the tree, we decorate. Or, more accurately, Georgie throws tinsel at the branches with reckless abandon, while Callum and I try to make the ornaments look intentional.

"Careful with that one, Georgie," Callum says, gesturing to an ornament she's holding. "It's

glass."

"Got it!" she says, placing it gingerly on a branch before immediately grabbing another handful of tinsel.

"This one's from when I was a kid," I say, holding up a slightly chipped ceramic star. "Made it in kindergarten. Nana Barbie insists it goes on the tree every year, even though it looks like a crime scene."

Callum squints at it. "Is that… supposed to be Santa?"

"Supposed to be." I hang it proudly in the center of the tree. "It's abstract."

He laughs, shaking his head.

"What about you, Charles?" Georgie pipes in. "What was Christmas like when you were little?"

"Loud," I say immediately, grinning at the memories that roll through my mind. "The house was always just plain chaos. My mom would bake enough cookies to feed an army, Dad would drag us to every tree lot in town, and my brothers and I would have snowball fights that always ended with someone crying."

"Who cried the most?" Georgie asked, sounding as genuinely concerned as her little six-year-old heart can manage.

"Alfie," I say, with Callum guessing right along with me, and I can't help but laugh that he knows my family so well already.

Georgie giggles at us before asking, "What about you, Daddy?"

Callum's smile falters just a little, and I can see the hesitation in his eyes. He doesn't talk about his childhood or much about life before Georgie came along.

"Well," he starts, adjusting a snowflake ornament. "When I was a kid, it was mostly just Sarah and me. We'd watch movies, eat junk food, and open presents early because we couldn't wait." The truth of no one being there to tell them no, or possibly even not having presents, goes unspoken, but I can read it clearly in his eyes.

"That sounds like a good time," I say softly, reaching out and running my hand comfortingly over his shoulder and down his arm, grabbing his hand and giving it a supportive squeeze.

"It was." He glances at Georgie, his expression softening. "And now it's even better because I have you."

Georgie beams, throwing her arms around his waist, but he scoops her into a big bear hug. She loops her arms around his neck, giving him her tightest squeeze.

"Daddy's a big softie," she whispers loudly over his shoulder.

"I won't tell if you don't," I whisper back.

Georgie giggles and quickly wriggles her way out of her father's arms, returning to her work on the tree. Callum twists and meets my eyes, watching me with a soft smile, and for a moment, I forget there's a tree in the room at all.

"What?" I ask, straightening up.

"Nothing," he says quickly, but his eyes give him away.

"Oh, it's something," I counter, stepping closer. "Spill it."

He sighs, running a hand through his hair. "It's just… this. All of it. The decorations, the tree, the whole thing. It's not something I've been great at, you know? Making traditions."

"What are you talking about? You're like Dad of the Year."

"Hardly." He laughs, but it's tinged with self-deprecation. "After Georgie's mom and I split, I tried to keep up with our traditions, but it felt... forced. Like I was trying too hard to make it perfect for her, and I was failing anyway."

"You weren't failing," I say immediately.

"How do you know?"

"Because, look at her," I nod toward Georgie, who's now wrapping the tree in ribbon with the determination of a professional interior designer. "That kid is happy, confident, and thinks glitter is a personality trait. That's all you."

He looks down, his jaw tight. "I don't know. Sometimes I feel like I'm just winging it."

"Newsflash: we're all winging it." I reach out, lacing my fingers with his. "But you're doing it with so much heart. She doesn't need perfect. She just needs you."

For a moment, the only sound in the room is Georgie singing *Jingle Bells* off-key. Callum squeezes my hand, his expression softening.

"Thanks, Charlie."

"Always." Before he can argue again, I lean in and press a kiss to his temple, taking a moment to savor this moment and his fresh, crisp scent.

"Okay, Daddy!" Georgie announces suddenly, spinning around and pulling us from our stolen moment. "What's next?"

Callum glances at the tree, then at me. "I think we're ready for the grand finale."

I grin, holding up the tree topper—a vintage-style star I picked up at a flea market years ago. "You want to do the honors, George?"

"Yes!" She bounces on her toes, reaching for it.

I lift her onto my shoulders, and she squeals with delight

as I carry her to the tree. Callum steadies the star as she places it on top, her face lit up with excitement.

"Perfect," I say, stepping back to admire our handiwork. The tree is a little chaotic, a little crooked, and absolutely perfect.

Later that night, after Georgie's been tucked into bed, Callum and I are sprawled on the couch, the glow of the tree lights casting soft shadows on the walls.

"You know," I say, resting my head against his shoulder, "this might be the best tree I've ever had."

"It's definitely the most colorful," he says, smiling down at me.

"Colorful's good."

"Yeah. It is."

I tilt my head, studying him. Something in his expression —something warm and unguarded—makes my chest ache in the best way.

"You're thinking too hard," I say softly.

"Am I?"

"Mm-hmm." I shift closer, sliding my hand over his. "What's on your mind?"

He hesitates, then lets out a breath. "Just… how different this year feels. In a good way. I never thought I'd have this—a house full of laughter, a tree full of memories… you."

My throat tightens, and I have to swallow hard before I can speak. "You deserve all of it, Callum. Every bit of happiness."

He turns to me, his gaze intent. "You make me believe that."

There's a pause, comfortable and warm, before he leans in and kisses me. It's soft at first, but when I slide my hand up to the back of his neck, he deepens it, and suddenly, the room feels a lot warmer than it did a minute ago.

"Charlie," he murmurs against my lips.

"Hmm?"

"You're distracting me."

"That's the idea."

He laughs, low and husky, before pulling me closer. And just like that, the rest of the world melts away, leaving only us and the twinkle of Christmas lights.

CHAPTER FOUR

CALLUM

DECEMBER 11TH

I glance at the clock as Georgie chatters away in the back seat, her small hands flying along as she tells me about her day. School let out ten minutes ago, and she's already gone from telling me every minute detail about her day in class to talking about the topic she's been absolutely obsessed with for the last week: The Larson family Christmas.

"And Nana Barbie said we can make *all* the cookies, not just the regular ones. She wants to teach me to make a special cookie, too!"

"Oh, yeah? What one is that?" I ask, doing my best to engage and follow the rapid-fire stream of consciousness.

"Crum… croom… croom-cake-ah or something. I think. It's a hard word, Daddy, but they sounded nummy, and Nana Barbie said they were a family tradition, so I want to learn them too!" she says excitedly, not in the least bit deterred by the unintelligible word I am not even going to attempt to decipher.

"Sounds like fun!" is the best I can offer, not wanting anything to spoil her good mood.

"Yeah! And we're going to put up decorations and lights everywhere too! Charlie said their house looks like Santa's workshop exploded," Georgie giggles.

"That tracks," I say, pulling up to the curb in front of our apartment building. It's hard not to smile as I watch her hop out of the car and bound up the front steps. Seeing her this excited about the holidays makes a sense of contentment wash over me. For years, Christmas was just the two of us, quiet and simple—more out of necessity than choice. Being a single father is no joke. But this year? This year feels different.

I follow her inside, dropping my keys on the counter when we enter our apartment. Georgie flings her backpack onto the floor and immediately starts digging through it.

"Homework?" I ask, raising an eyebrow. Seriously. She's in first grade. Why the hell do six-year-olds need to do this much homework?

"Worksheets," she replies, already groaning as she pulls her take-home folder from her bag.

"You'll survive," I encourage her, ruffling her curls as I walk into the living room.

"Maybe." She drags her backpack over to the small dining table, then pauses, looking up at me. "Do you think Nana Barbie will let me taste the frosting while we bake?"

"Knowing her? Absolutely."

Her answering grin is so wide it's contagious.

Later, after Georgie finishes her homework, helps with dinner cleanup, and subsequently disappears into her room to play before bedtime, I settle onto the couch with my laptop to get a little work done. Charlie's working a closing shift at the brewery tonight, and it's almost startling to realize how quickly he has become a part of our daily routines and how quiet the apartment is without him. I'm not sure I like it. The him not being here with us, that is, not the quiet part. That I kind of love since I get so few moments of it anymore.

I'm scrolling through emails when my phone buzzed on the armrest. I glance at the screen and smile. "Hey, stranger," I say, answering the call.

"Hey yourself," Sarah replies, her voice warm but laced with that familiar little sister sass. "How're my two favorite humans?"

"Good. Really good, actually. Gearing up for Christmas, as ya do. Georgie's been counting down the days since Thanksgiving. She and Betha made a paper chain to hang in her room and everything. It's a big deal to tear off another link every night before bed now," I explain with a tired chuckle. I love doing things like this with Georgie and making these memories. That doesn't make them any less exhausting, though.

"Sounds like fun," Sarah says. "What about you? How's... you know, everything with Charlie?"

I can practically hear the smirk in her voice, and I roll my eyes. "Everything's great. He's great. And no, he still hasn't come to his senses and gone back to being straight, you brat," I say with exasperation. I love my sister, but no one drives me as crazy as she does.

"Good. I'm glad to hear that," she replies with a weird amount of self-satisfaction. As if my response absolved her of some sisterly duty to kick his ass or something.

"What about you? How's life in Denver?"

There's a pause before she answers that sets my spidey-senses tingling. "It's fine. Work's busy, as usual. And, uh, Christmas is looking pretty quiet this year."

I frown, her words catching me off guard. "Quiet? What about your friends? Or that guy you were seeing?"

"Oh, you mean the one who decided commitment wasn't his thing?" she says dryly. "Yeah, he's out of the picture. And most of my friends are traveling to see their families, so it's just me this year. Alone. In my very quiet apartment."

"Sarah…"

"Don't start," she says, cutting me off before I can go full big-brother mode. "It's not a big deal. I've got a stack of books and some wine. I'll survive."

I glance toward Georgie's room and sigh. The thought of Sarah spending Christmas alone makes my chest tighten, but I know better than to push her. She's always been fiercely independent; the last thing she wants or will accept from me is pity.

"You know you're always welcome here," I say carefully, keeping my tone light. "If you change your mind."

"I know," she says softly. "But you've got your hands full with Georgie, Charlie, and the rest of his crazy brood. I wouldn't want to crash the party."

"You wouldn't be crashing anything," I say, but don't push further.

"I'll think about it," she says after a moment. "Maybe next year."

"Okay," I say, letting it drop. "But seriously, if you change your mind, just say the word."

"Got it," she says, and I can hear the smile in her voice. "Now, tell me more about these Larsons. Are they as over the top as they sound?"

"Worse," I say, laughing.

———

AFTER I HANG UP, I sit for a moment, staring at the darkened screen of my phone. Sarah's always been the type to downplay her feelings, but I can't shake the sense that she's lonelier than she's letting on.

"You okay, Daddy?" Georgie asks, coming back into the room and crawling onto the couch next to me.

"Yeah, sweetie," I say, forcing a smile. "Just thinking about Auntie Sarah."

"Why?" she asks, innocently blinking up at me.

"Well, it's the first Christmas we've been in Minnesota, so she's back in Denver by herself, and she doesn't have any big plans."

Georgie frowns, her little brows furrowing. "That's not fair. Christmas is supposed to be fun."

"It is," I agree. "But sometimes grown-ups have quieter holidays."

She doesn't look convinced, but she lets it go, settling into the cushions and snagging the remote to watch a show like we usually do before the bedtime routine kicks in every night.

Once she's settled, I stand and putter around the living room and kitchen, straightening from the day. As I work, I can't shake the thought of Sarah spending Christmas alone. I know she's strong enough to handle it, but part of me wants to grab her and drag her here, kicking and screaming if necessary. We spent enough holidays growing up in empty houses with no real Christmas cheer; there is no reason for her to still be doing it now. Maybe I should see if I could take a few days and head to her. I don't like taking time off, especially during the holidays, but this is eating at me.

"Hey, Daddy?" Georgie calls from the living room, her voice bright with curiosity.

"Yeah?" I ask, stepping out from behind the kitchen counter.

"Do you think Auntie Sarah likes cookies?"

I laugh, remembering when Sarah was in middle school and all but lived on Oreos and energy drinks. "I think she loves them."

Georgie's eyes light up with that mischievous light that always worries me. "Then maybe we should make her some. Just in case she changes her mind."

I grin, crossing to the couch and pressing a kiss to the top of her head. "You're a good kid, you know that?"

"I know," she says, beaming.

CHAPTER FIVE

CHARLIE

DECEMBER 14TH

Walking down Main Street in the growing twilight, the air smells like spices, pine, and a hint of roasted chestnuts. Though I have no idea if anyone's actually roasting chestnuts or, honestly, what a chestnut even looks like, but the holiday magic is strong tonight either way. I glance down at Georgie, who's practically vibrating with excitement, her mittens clutched in mine and Callum's hands as she swings them between us.

"Look at all the lights, Charlie!" she squeals, bouncing on her toes as we weave through the crowd gathered for the annual tree lighting and Christmas market. The entire stretch of the business district on Main Street is strung with lights crisscrossing the road, which has been blocked off to cars for the evening for the event to allow for the increased foot traffic. The street is lined with pop-up tents, vendors, and specialty booths, leading to the massive Christmas tree set up in the roundabout square where the road dead-ends in front of Spirit of Hops and Valkyrie bar before leading into the small riverfront park.

"I see them," I say, smiling down at her. "Pretty sure the lights see you, too. You're shining brighter than half of them tonight, short stuff."

She giggles, her cheeks pink from the cold and probably the three marshmallows she managed to swipe from the hot chocolate stand Alfie is manning in front of the coffee shop at the top of the hill tonight. Callum chuckles next to me, a soft, indulgent smile on his face as he glances at me over her bouncing little head.

The market is packed tonight with, I swear, at least three-quarters of the town's residents, all bundled up in puffy coats and scarves, holding steaming cups of cocoa or cider. Vendors sell everything from handmade ornaments, crafts, wreaths, and special gift baskets from all the various shops and businesses in town. Carolers are stationed near the massive tree, harmonizing *O Holy Night* like they've been training for this moment their whole lives.

Georgie stops abruptly, nearly yanking my arm from its socket, and screeches, "There's the cookie tent!"

She's pointing at a white tent in the brewery parking lot with a banner that says *Holiday Cookie Wonderland* across it. Emily is standing out front dressed as an elf and directing the little kids and overwhelmed parents. Inside, tables are piled high with sugar cookies, tubs of frosting, and enough candy decorations to send any dentist into an early retirement.

"You hear her, Cal," I tease. "The lady has spoken."

Callum shoots me a look—half exasperated, half amused. "You're lucky you're cute," he mutters.

"Alright, sugar queen," I say, clapping my hands on her shoulders and steering her toward the tent. "Let's see what you've got."

Waving to Emily as we pass into the tent, we're smacked in the face by the smell of sugar so thick in the air it's like walking through a candy fog. The three of us claim spots at a table, and Georgie immediately gets to work, slathering a cookie with enough green frosting to make it unrecognizable. Callum sits next to her, pretending to guide her but clearly just sneaking bits of candy into his mouth when he thinks I'm not looking.

"Caught you," I say, flicking a red sprinkle at him as I sit across from them.

He smirks, popping a gumdrop into his mouth. "Gotta taste test. Quality assurance."

"Daddy, look!" Georgie's voice carries over the hum of the crowd.

Callum leans closer, watching her work over her shoulder. "Is that supposed to be a … reindeer? Or…" he leads, his voice uncertain but doing his best not to have her catch on.

"A unicorn!" Georgie declares proudly, holding up the most chaotic cookie I have ever seen.

I lean closer, pretending to inspect it. "Hmm. I think that unicorn has seen some things," I murmur out the side of my mouth toward him.

Georgie giggles, slapping more sprinkles onto the poor thing. "It's magical!"

"Sure is, kiddo," Cal says, ruffling her hair.

The entire scene is warm and sweet in a way I never thought I'd get to experience. It's been years since Christmas felt this full, this alive… and that's saying something considering the insanity that is my family on any given day, but especially around the holidays. Watching Callum and Georgie together, getting to be part of their moments, I can't help but feel like the luckiest man alive.

"Hey," Cal says, nudging me under the table with his boot. "You okay? You're staring."

"Can't a guy admire his incredibly handsome and sexy boyfriend once in a while?"

Callum smirks, a hint of a blush creeping onto his cheeks. "Flattery will get you everywhere, but not in public, you heathen."

"Noted," I tease, waggling my eyebrows ridiculously at him.

By the time we leave the tent, Georgie is clutching a small bag of her creations, and I'm pretty sure half the icing ended up on her gloves.

"Caroling next!" she declares, pointing toward the group gathered around the base of the massive tree.

"Lead the way, boss," I say, tipping an imaginary hat. Cal and I follow her through the crowd, joining the group as they launch into *Deck the Halls*. Georgie sings loud, proud, and slightly off-key, her little voice carrying over the sea of adults around her. Callum joins in, too, his voice low and warm, like melted caramel wrapping itself around me and distracting the hell out of me, leaving me struggling to keep up with the lyrics as I fight a blush.

The next hour is a blur of slightly off-key signing, marshmallow roasting, and an impromptu snowball fight that Georgie starts, but I am not ashamed to admit Callum wins—though only because I was too busy laughing to defend myself and fight off a sneak attack appearance from my brother. Ollie ducked out of the booth he had set up in front of his tattoo shop, where he and his artists were doing face painting for the kids and temporary tattoos for teenagers and adults just long enough to shove a fist full of snow down the back of my shirt like the little shit he is.

By the time the tree lighting is about to start, we're all rosy-cheeked and breathless from the cold and laughing. The crowd gathers around the massive tree, which is easily twenty feet tall and covered in what feels like miles of twinkling lights.

"Are you ready?" Georgie asks, bouncing on the balls of her feet.

"Ready," I say, pulling her close to keep her warm, feeling Callum slot in next to us, his arm setting casually around my waist.

The mayor steps up to a podium and launches into a speech that no one listens to or cares about as we all wait impatiently for the main event. When he finally finishes with a flourish, the countdown begins.

"Ten... nine..."

Georgie joins in, jumping up and almost landing on my toes with every number she screams out over the crowd.

"Three... two... one!"

The tree bursts to life, lights cascading down its branches in a kaleidoscope of colors and reflecting off the hundreds of glass ornaments in all shapes and sizes. The crowd erupts into cheers, and I glance down at Georgie, whose face is lit with pure, unfiltered, childish wonder.

"Wow," she whispers, her eyes wide as she takes it all in.

"It's pretty magical," I say softly to no one in particular.

"Not bad," Callum adds, gently squeezing my waist. "But you're still the most magical thing I've seen all night, Charlie Larson."

"Cheesy," I mutter, but I can't stop the grin that spreads across my face.

"Worth it," he says, leaning in.

And then, right there under the glow of the tree, and in front of the whole damn town, my man kisses me. It's soft and sweet, a kiss that feels like home. No matter how many times I feel the warm press of his lips against mine, the soft scrape of his beard, it still makes my heart do that ridiculous fluttering thing whenever he's near.

When we pull back, Georgie is watching us with the kind of expression that only a six-year-old can pull off—a mix of approval and mild disgust.

"Ew," she says, but she's smiling. "You guys are so mushy."

"Get used to it, George," I say, tugging at one dangling end of her brightly colored hat. She rolls her eyes dramatically but grabs our hands, pulling us toward the next activity.

As we walk through the glowing market, laughter echoing around us and snow beginning to fall, I realize that this—messy, chaotic, and utterly perfect—is exactly what Christmas is supposed to feel like. And I will do anything and everything in my power to never let it, or them, go.

CHAPTER SIX

CALLUM

DECEMBER 18TH

There's something about the hum of the busy brewery that feels familiar and comforting now that I have settled into my role here at Spirit of Hops over the last few months. The clinking of glasses, the low murmur of conversation, the occasional burst of laughter—it's a rhythm I love, especially when it's underscored by the sight of Charlie behind the bar, moving with an effortless grace I find undeniably sexy.

Georgie and I have claimed a table near the back, close enough to the action for her to people-watch but far enough away that I don't have to worry about her getting underfoot when it's busier like this and bar-top seating is at a premium. She's tucked into the corner across from me, sipping hot cocoa from a special Santa mug one of the girls – either Sloan or Emily, most likely—got special for her, and Charlie keeps behind the bar for when she comes to visit because *"it's the holidays, Callum, and we're festive, damn it."*

"Is Charlie always this busy?" she asks, watching as he pours a beer with one hand while ringing up another tab with the other, and keeping up a conversation with a regular sitting at the bar behind him.

Sexy. As. Hell. I have competency kink. So sue me.

"Pretty much," I answer her, leaning back in my chair to get a better view.

Georgie sighs into her mug like that is the most disappointing thing she has ever heard. The chocolate mustache on her upper lip ruins the disgruntled-mein and really only makes her look that much more adorable. "Can I help him?" she asks after watching him for another long moment.

I shake my head, leaning back in toward her. "Maybe when you're taller. And older. And have a permit or something."

She huffs but doesn't argue, her attention shifting to the holiday decorations Emily and Sloan insisted on putting up, apparently like they do every year, much to Luka's consternation—also like every year. Twinkling lights are strung across the ceiling beams, a massive wreath hangs behind the bar, and swags of garland hang from every available space and leading up the stairs toward the offices, adding to the cozy vibe.

"Georgie," Charlie calls from behind the bar, his hands still busy pouring two different mugs, but his attention seemingly fully on her. "I need your help. We've got a crisis on our hands!"

Her eyes go wide. "What kind of crisis?" she calls over the din of the patrons, springing up from her seat and rushing toward the bar. Charlie leans across the bar top conspiratorially when she reaches it and scrambles up onto an open stool. He whispers something to her, and I watch as she nods vigorously in response, her blond curls bouncing wildly before Charlie slides a bowl of pretzels her way with a wink and returns to pulling pints.

Watching them together does something to my chest. Seeing how effortlessly Charlie includes her in his world makes me feel like I've hit some kind of emotional jackpot or won some cosmic lottery. Georgie deserves this—someone who sees her as more than just "my kid" and treats her like the brilliant, curious little bundle of awesome that she is.

While they are distracted with their top-secret mission, I nurse my beer and let myself relax, taking a moment to breathe and enjoy a somewhat quiet moment amid the craziness that is this month. It's one of the rare moments where everything just feels... right.

And then the door behind me opens, a blast of cold air pulling my attention, and my sister Sarah walks in, a massive duffle bag-purse-thing slung over one shoulder.

I blink, wondering if I've somehow conjured her out of thin air. "Sarah?"

"Surprise!" she calls, turning to me with a bright smile as she pulls off her hat and shakes out her hair.

Hearing her shout, Georgie whips around on her seat, her eyes lighting up, and she's off her stool in a flash, running toward her aunt. Sarah scoops her up, spinning her around before setting her down with a laugh.

"What're you doing here?" I ask, getting to my feet.

Sarah shrugs, her smile widening. "I figured Christmas alone in Denver sounded boring. Besides, I missed you guys. Thought I'd crash the party."

"You didn't even call," I say, but I can't hide my smile.

"Where's the fun in that?"

"Charles!" Georgie yells, jumping up and down and waving her arms over her head to get his attention. "Look who's here!"

Charlie's face lights up when he sees her, and he slips out

from behind the bar and makes a beeline toward us. "Sarah! Welcome to the madness!" he calls as he reaches us, his arms open wide, offering a hug.

"Thanks!" Sarah says, stepping in to accept a quick hug from him. "I figured it was time to meet the guy who's been making my brother all googly-eyed."

"I'm not googly-eyed," I mutter, and she raises an eyebrow.

"Cal, you're practically a cartoon heart with legs at this point," she says, smirking.

Charlie just laughs, slipping an arm around my waist and grinning at me. "Guilty as charged and not the least bit sorry about it."

I can't help but laugh at his response and lean in to steal a kiss. I have every intention of keeping it quick and PG, but, like he so often does, Charlie draws me closer. I lose myself in him for a moment, only pulled back to reality by the sound of both Sarah and Georgie making overdramatic retching and gagging sounds next to us, and we all break into gut-wrenching laughter.

Charlie waves at Emily, the other bartender working tonight, letting her know where he will be if she needs him before we all settle back at my table. Georgie bounces out of her seat as Sarah settles next to her, telling us about her spur-of-the-moment decision to visit. She talks about how quiet things have been in Denver and jokes about needing a break from her cooking, making Georgie laugh so hard she snorts.

Sarah launches into a story about her drive up from Denver... why the hell she drove instead of flying, I will never understand. Apparently, she hit a snowstorm, got lost twice, and had to bribe a gas station attendant with leftover pumpkin pie to find her way back to the main road.

"You brought pie on a road trip?" I ask, incredulous.

"Priorities, Cal," she says, deadpan.

I'm about to respond when the door opens again, and Donnie strolls in. He's in his usual work attire—blue mechanic's coveralls tied at the waist, work boots, and a surprisingly crisp white tank under a flannel shirt left hanging open and rolled up at the sleeves, looking like he just stepped off a blue-collar calendar shoot. He heads straight for the bar, nodding at Charlie as he passes our group, but when his gaze lands on Sarah, he stops mid-step.

"Hey Donnie," I call, waving him over.

He approaches, his expression shifting from casual to intrigued as his eyes flick between me and Sarah.

"Sarah, this is Donnie—one of Charlie's brothers. Donnie, my sister, Sarah," I say, gesturing between them.

"Nice to meet you," Donnie says, his voice warm as he offers her a handshake.

"You too," Sarah replies, and there's a moment—a beat too long for polite introductions—where they're just looking at each other.

Ever the observer, Georgie tilts her head like she's watching something fascinating. I can practically see the gears turning in her little brain.

"So, what brings you to town?" Donnie asks, pulling up a chair.

"Decided to shake things up," Sarah says, her tone light but her smile a little shy.

"Well, you picked the right place," he says. "We do chaos pretty well here."

Sarah laughs, and just like that, they're off, trading jokes and stories like they've known each other for years.

I glance at Charlie, sitting next to me with an arm draped casually across the back of my chair, and who's watching them with the same curious expression I most likely have. "They're hitting it off," he murmurs, leaning close.

"Too soon to say," I reply, but my eyes flick back to Georgie, who's excitedly watching the two of them.

Before anything more can happen, a large group pours through the door, and Emily calls Charlie back behind the bar to help manage the crowd. Donnie, falling back on his usual loner 'man of mystery' ways, makes his excuses before retreating to the bar as well. Sarah and I catch up some more while Georgie draws and colors snowmen on the back of a coaster.

"So," I say, giving her a knowing look after catching her looking over at the bar for the hundredth time in the last ten minutes.

She smirks. "What?"

"Don't '*what*' me," I say. "I saw that."

"Saw what?" she asks, feigning innocence.

"You and Donnie," I say, lowering my voice. "There were… sparks."

Sarah rolls her eyes. "Please. We were just talking."

"Uh-huh," I answer, smirking. My sister just rolls her eyes before turning back to Georgie and joining in on the coloring.

As the night winds down and we're getting ready to leave, Georgie tugs on my sleeve while I help her into her coat.

"Daddy," she whispers, her eyes sparkling with mischief. "I think Auntie Sarah and Uncle Donnie should get married."

I choke on my laugh, trying not to draw attention. "That's… a little fast, don't ya think?"

"They like each other," she insists, crossing her arms. "And I'm a romance expert."

"Georgie, not everyone who likes each other gets married," I say, but her determined expression tells me this is not the end of the conversation.

She leans in conspiratorially. "It could be their Christmas present!"

I sigh, pressing a kiss to her forehead. "We'll see, sweetheart."

But as we finish getting our coats on and settle the tab, Sarah and Donnie exchange another lingering look, and I can't help but wonder if Georgie's little matchmaking project might not be as far-fetched after all.

As our little group steps out into the crisp, snowy night air, Sarah wraps her arm around my shoulders while Charlie and Georgie chase each other around the patio and toward the nearly empty parking lot. "Thanks for letting me crash your holiday plans," she says softly.

"Are you kidding?" I say, pulling her closer. "Christmas wouldn't be the same without you."

And as Georgie and Charlie skip ahead, humming a Christmas carol together, I can't help but feel like this holiday season is shaping up to be something truly special.

CHAPTER SEVEN

CHARLIE

DECEMBER 20TH

If my family gatherings were a Christmas movie, they'd fall somewhere between *National Lampoon's Christmas Vacation* and *Home Alone*. A solid mix of chaos, charm, and potential for bodily harm and flying paint cans. Don't believe me? Ask Alfie about the 'Christmas Pageant incident of '02' and watch how red he turns.

I have to keep that in mind as Callum and I do our best to reassure Sarah for the hundredth time that tagging along isn't a giant mistake on her part.

"Are you *sure* you're sure this is a good idea?" she asks from the passenger seat, glancing nervously at the poinsettia she insisted on bringing as a hostess gift for my mom.

"You're overthinking it," I say, glancing over at her as I pull up to a stop sign. I swear her nervous energy is rubbing off on me, damn it. "My family collects strays like Georgie collects stuffies. You'll fit right in. And with that present, you'll be her favorite before the rest of us even get through the door."

"Is that supposed to be comforting?" she deadpans, but there's a smile tugging at the corner of her mouth. It's an improvement, at least.

From the backseat, Georgie pipes up. "Auntie Sarah, you *have* to come!" she declares, throwing her arms out dramatically and smacking Callum in the arm in the seat next to her. "It wouldn't feel like Christmas without you!"

"See?" I say, shooting Sarah a quick, reassuring smile. "If Georgie says it, it's law."

Sarah shakes her head but finally relents with a smile. "Fine. But if they're as over-the-top as you've warned me, I'm holding you personally responsible for my sanity."

"Deal," I reply. "Though I make no promises," I tease with a wink as I pull into my parents' place, parking behind my brothers' trucks, already clogging the driveway.

The Larson house smells and looks like Christmas exploded inside it. The scent of roasting ham mingles with cinnamon candles, fresh pine from the not one, not two, but *three* real trees my mother has crammed into the house this year, and every available surface is decked out with garlands, snow globes, snow village houses, and at least one animatronic Santa playing *Jingle Bells* on repeat.

"Charlie! Callum! Georgie!" my mom exclaims, pulling us into a group hug as soon as we step inside. She notices Sarah hanging back and gasps, shoving between us unceremoniously on her way to her next victim. "You must be Sarah! Oh, you're lovely, just lovely! Callum, you didn't tell me your sister was so adorable!"

"Uh, thanks?" Sarah stammers, blinking at us over Mom's shoulder.

"Come in, come in! Georgie's been talking about you nonstop. And don't worry about a thing."

"O…okay," Sarah says, trying her best to keep up with the whirlwind that is Nana Barbie. "Um, this is for you, Mrs. Larson," she offers, holding out the poinsettia still clasped in her hands like a lifeline.

I swear my mom's heart melts, and I am pretty sure I see her tear up as she takes the plant from Sarah's hands and pulls her into another hug. "Thank you, sweet girl! It's perfect. And none of that Mrs. Larson nonsense. It's Barbie, or Nana Barbie, if you like. You're family now."

It's hard to argue with Nana Barbie when she's in full hostess mode. Sarah is whisked away and into the kitchen before I can offer any kind of lifeline, leaving us to hang up the coats.

"She's not going to escape for hours," I whisper to Cal as we help Georgie out of her coat before she dashes off, disappearing deeper into the house.

"She'll survive," he says with a grin. "Your mom's not *that* scary."

"You only say that because you've never been cornered by her at 2 a.m. with a box of condoms and a banana ready for *the talk* after you stumbled home from a horrible date," I mutter, and Callum just laughs.

The dining room is in peak chaos when we walk in. Chairs scrape across the floor as Alfie and Ollie argue over who has to carve the ham—which is pointless because that has always been and will always be Dad's job—and Donnie is attempting to balance three plates of sides while Mom yells at him to "just let your brothers help!" In the middle of it all stands Georgie, clipboard in hand (where the hell did she get a clipboard?), directing traffic like she's in charge of a holiday-themed airport.

"Georgie," I say, cautiously approaching and ducking a stray roll lobbed by one of my brothers toward the other. I'm not really sure who threw it or why at this point, but it's just par for the course for one of our family dinners. "What's with the clipboard?"

"I'm organizing the seating chart," she answers, her tone all business as she consults the crayon scribbles on her sheet. "It's very important."

I raise an eyebrow at Callum, and he leans in. "She's matchmaking," he whispers.

I bite back a laugh, looking over to where Sarah and Donnie linger near the far end of the table. "Is this… about them?"

"It's always about them the last few days," he says. "She's been plotting since Sarah showed up at the brewery." Callum sighs but doesn't intervene. Honestly, who has the energy to outmaneuver a six-year-old these days?

By the time everyone sits down, Sarah and Donnie are miraculously seated side-by-side, and Georgie is beaming like the little evil mastermind she is. Dinner kicks off with the usual chaotic energy of a Larson family meal: overlapping conversations, exaggerated stories, and enough teasing to make any outsider question their life choices.

At one point, after Alfie and Ollie almost come to blows over the gravy boat, Callum leans closer to me with an equally amused and terrified look. "We really didn't prepare Sarah for this, did we?"

"She's a quick study," I say, watching Sarah exchange a bemused glance with Donnie. "She's holding her own just fine."

"So, Callum," my mom drawls about halfway through the meal, dragging out the 'o' and ignoring the insanity of her sons in classic mom fashion, fixing Cal with a smile that's both affectionate and mischievous. "How's my Charlie doing as a boyfriend? Keeping you happy?"

Callum chokes on his drink, and I groan, sinking in my chair. "Mooooom…"

"What?" she blinks back at me, feigning innocence. "I'm just curious!"

Meddling, no-good woman.

"He's perfect," Callum says once she's regained his composure, his hand finding mine under the table. "I couldn't ask for better."

This man. This fucking man. I swear I don't know what I did to deserve him, but I will thank every deity and spirit who will listen for him every damn day as long as I can keep him by my side.

"Oh fer cute!" Mom coos, clasping her hands together under her chin like a schoolgirl. "Isn't that just the sweetest thing you've ever heard?"

"Gross," Ollie mutters, in the way only a youngest brother can, earning a sharp elbow from Alife as Sarah makes a gagging noise and mimes choking herself on a finger, triggering Donnie to snort-laugh mid-drink and narrowly avoid sending his wine through his nose.

"Don't be jealous," Alfie teases. "Some of us just have more charm than others."

"Charm, huh?" Ollie replies with an evil smirk. "I seem to recall you tripping over your own feet at the coffee shop the other day. How is the lovely Anya, by the way?"

"Okay, let's not revisit the dark ages," Alfie says quickly, ducking his head and avoiding meeting anyone's eyes as the table erupts into laughter.

Despite the teasing, there's no denying the warmth that fills the room. My parents preside over the craziness with practiced grace, ensuring everyone has enough to eat and no one's glass stays empty for long.

As the meal winds down and people push back from the table, too stuffed to even look at another bite of food and needing the extra space for the food babies we are all sporting now, Dad stands to make a toast.

"Before we all slip into food comas," he begins, his voice warm and steady, "I just want to say how grateful I am to have you all here tonight."

The room quiets, all of us giving Dad our full attention, a rare occurrence in this house.

"Family is what makes the holidays special," he continues. "So here's to family," he says, raising his glass. "Whether it's the family we've been born into or the ones that found us." He glances meaningfully at Callum, Georgie, and even Sarah, which causes my chest to tighten. These two, now three, truly have become my family in the last few months, and seeing the rest of my family accept them so readily and wholeheartedly means everything to me.

There's a beat of quiet, everyone raising their glasses in silent agreement, and then Mom chimes in. "And to whoever's doing the dishes tonight!" she declares, breaking the poignant but heavy moment with a wide smile. Laughter erupts, and just like that, the chaos resumes.

Once none of us can possibly fit another bite of food in our faces, we all help clear the table of dinner to make room for the eventual dessert, albeit slowly and with plenty of grunts and groans of protest. As we help stack the last of the dishes for my brothers to carry into the kitchen, I catch Callum watching me with an expression that's equal parts amused and fond.

"What?" I ask, doubling up the stack of plates and handing it off to Ollie, who just grumbles and shuffles back toward the kitchen, cursing my name under his breath as he goes.

"Nothing," Cal says, smiling softly at me. "Just… you're really good at this."

"At what?"

"This. Family. Being… a part of it all."

I glance around the room and down the short hall toward

the kitchen, the laughter and chatter of my family filling every corner. "They make it easy."

"Still," he says, leaning in to brush his lips over mine in a soft kiss. "I'm glad we're here."

"Me too," I reply, and mean it. Sliding my arm around his waist, I tug him against me and deepen the kiss. We can hear the rest of the family still causing a ruckus in the other room, but I can't find it in myself to care. I want to enjoy this stolen moment with the man I love.

I can't help the soft moan that escapes as Cal deepens the kiss, sinking into my arms and wrapping his around my neck. The kiss is slow and sweet, and so full of love and affection—everything we both need in this moment.

Cal's fingers brush through the hair at the nape of my neck, sending a shiver down my spine and pulling another moan from me. "I'm so fucking lucky," I whisper against his lips.

"Pretty sure I am getting the better end of this deal," Cal chuckles between teasing kisses.

"You know I love you, right?" I ask. Already knowing the answer, but never one to miss a chance to hear him say it; I'm a greedy motherfucker like that.

"Love you, too," Cal replies, leaning his forehead against mine. We stay quietly sharing breath and wrapped in each other's arms, just enjoying the stolen moment.

"Callum! Your daughter is bound for the mafia, I swear!" Alfie hollers from the kitchen, making us laugh and breaking the delicate bubble of our moment. Taking Callum's hand in mine, we walk into the kitchen and join the chaos again. Even as mom scolds Ollie for leaving fingerprints on her freshly washed china, and Georgie and Sarah conspire about who-knows-what in the corner, I can't imagine being anywhere else.

CHAPTER EIGHT

CALLUM

DECEMBER 20TH

The Larson house after dinner is a unique kind of insanity that's strangely comforting. Dishes clatter in the kitchen, laughter spills from the dining room, and it's all underscored by the smell of pie and coffee. It's like being wrapped in a very noisy, slightly sticky hug, and unlike any holiday I have ever experienced.

I'm leaning against the kitchen counter, nursing a cup of coffee, when I notice Sarah still seated at the table with Donnie, though they have migrated into the far corner to stay out of traffic lanes. Most of the family is still in the kitchen helping with cleanup or has migrated to the living room for dessert. However, those two are still locked in conversation, their voices low and companionable.

Sarah's laughing—really laughing, the kind that makes her shoulders shake—and I can't help but smile. She's been holding her own tonight, which isn't easy when you're dropped into an absolute circus like this family, especially coming from a background like ours.

Charlie appears at my side, sliding an arm around my waist and brushing a soft kiss against the nape of my neck. "Look at them," he says, nodding toward our siblings. "Georgie's going to take all the credit for this, you know."

"She deserves some," I admit. "That seating arrangement was no accident, as you well know."

Charlie chuckles. "You think Donnie caught on?"

"Doubt it," I say, watching as Donnie gestures animatedly, probably recounting some crazy story from their childhood. Sarah is hanging on every word, her expression a mix of amusement and curiosity. "He's too busy trying to impress her."

"Smart man," Charlie says with a grin.

Barbie calls for Charlie from the other room, and as he leaves, I can't resist the brotherly urge to snoop on my sister. I move closer to the door to the dining room, pretending to tidy up while keeping an ear on their conversation.

"I can't imagine growing up with five of you in the house," Sarah says, her voice light and teasing. She's got that half-smile that means she's genuinely interested in what he has to say.

"Yep," Donnie replies. "Growing up, our house was basically a mix between a wrestling ring and a circus. Eddie, the prodigal brother who isn't here tonight, once set his shoelaces on fire to prove a point about friction or some-thing—while he was still wearing them."

Sarah blinks, then bursts out laughing. "What point was he trying to prove?"

"No idea," Donnie says, grinning. "Pretty sure he forgot halfway through and just committed to the bit. That's Eddie for ya, though."

Sarah looks at ease with him, her earlier hesitations about

crashing dinner all but forgotten. It's a good look on her—lighter, freer.

"Your family sounds wild," she says.

"Oh, we're wild, all right," Donnie says, leaning back in his chair, grinning like he's already won the lottery. "And you? What's life like in Denver? Snowball fights and wrestling matches galore?"

Sarah shakes her head, still smiling. "Not quite. It's quieter, but I like it. I've got my routine—work, yoga, the occasional weekend hike."

Donnie mock-winces. "Routine sounds dangerous. You survived dinner with us, though. I think you're ready for some more chaos in your life."

"Oh, is that so?" she says, raising an eyebrow.

"Absolutely," Donnie replies, utterly confident. "And if you're looking for recommendations, I know a loud, nosy family that's always hiring."

Sarah laughs again, and I catch Charlie's eye from across the room where he's walking in from the living room. He raises his eyebrows, clearly thinking the same thing I am: this has potential.

DESSERT IS EVENTUALLY SERVED in the living room, and somehow, the energy ramps up even more. Georgie sits cross-legged on the floor with a plate of cookies the size of her head while the rest of us squeeze onto the couches and armchairs scattered invitingly around the room. Someone suggests charades, and before I know it, we're dividing into teams.

"Sarah's on my team!" Ollie declares, grabbing her arm before she can protest.

She looks mildly alarmed but doesn't resist, glancing at me as if to say, *What have I gotten myself into?*

Before I can reassure her, Nana Barbie takes charge, armed with a timer and an endless supply of sass. "No cheating," she warns, glaring at Ollie.

"Why does she always look at me when she says that?" Ollie complains, tossing a marshmallow into his mouth.

"Because you always cheat, dumbass," Alfie deadpans, earning a smack upside the head from Joel and a round of laughter from the rest of us.

"Focus!" Barbie barks, pointing at the bowl of clues. "Callum, you're up!"

I groan but take my place at the front of the room, pulling a slip of paper from the bowl. "Okay, but no laughing at me. I suck at this game."

Georgie hollers, "I believe in you, Daddy!" while Charlie calls, "We make no promises," from the couch, his grin wide enough to make my stomach do that annoying flip-flop thing.

The clue is *Santa Claus*. Easy enough, right? Except as soon as I pantomime a jolly belly laugh, Georgie shouts, "A snowman eating spaghetti!" and the room descends into peels of laughter.

The next round starts with Alfie acting out *Titanic*, which involves an unfortunate attempt at recreating the "I'm the king of the world!" pose using an unsuspecting floor lamp. Sarah laughs so hard she has to wipe tears from her eyes, and I notice Donnie watching her, his smile soft.

Sarah, it turns out, is surprisingly good at charades. At first, she's a little hesitant, but by her second turn, she's fully committed. When she has to act out *Jurassic Park*, she stomps around the living room, her arms tucked in like T-Rex claws, while Donnie cheers her on with an entirely over-the-top enthusiasm.

"You've got this, Sarah!" he calls, offering her a dramatic thumbs up.

She breaks character long enough to laugh, then roars at him, sending the room into fits of laughter again.

"Dinosaur!" Georgie shouts immediately.

"Roaring?" I guess, trying to keep up.

Sarah flails her tiny arms and stomps around the room, and Georgie shrieks with laughter. "It's a T-Rex!"

"Close enough!" Sarah says, collapsing back onto the couch beside me in mock exhaustion.

"New rule," Ollie announces, wiping tears from his eyes. "Sarah has to come to every game night from now on."

"I second that," Nana Barbie says, raising her mug of cider like a gavel.

Donnie claps for Sarah like she's just won an Oscar. "See? I told you you could handle the chaos."

After a few more rounds, the evening winds down; the room growing quieter as the sugar rush of dessert is replaced by the inevitable crash. Dessert plates are stacked, Georgie's energy dips into that loopy, pre-bedtime phase, and the adults settle into softer conversations.

"Need a ride back?" Donnie asks Sarah casually, though his tone has just enough hesitation to suggest he's nervous.

"Oh, I don't want to put you out," Sarah says, though the smile tugging at her lips suggests she doesn't mind the offer.

"It's on my way," Donnie lies smoothly, and I have to bite back a laugh. I glance at Charlie, who raises an eyebrow at me like we're sharing a private joke. Donnie lives fifteen minutes in the opposite direction of my apartment where Sarah is staying.

Sarah hesitates, glancing at me as if looking for permission.

"It's fine," I say, keeping my tone light. "Donnie's a great chauffeur. He only makes you listen to one boy band song per trip."

"Hey, Backstreet Boys are timeless," Donnie protests, feigning offense.

Sarah smiles. "Okay, thanks. I appreciate it."

"Anytime," he replies, and for a moment, the two of them just stand there, smiling at each other.

Georgie tugs on my sleeve, whispering loudly enough for half the room to hear. "It's working, Daddy!"

"Georgie," I say gently, crouching to meet her eyes. "Sometimes these things take time. You can't rush people into–"

"I've *got this*," she interrupts, her confidence unwavering. "Trust me."

I glance over at Sarah and Donnie again, watching as he holds the front door open for her, and I can't help but think that maybe Georgie's right.

———

AFTER SEVERAL ROUNDS OF GOODBYES, a phenomenon I am told is called the *Minnesota Goodbye*, which cannot be completed in less than forty-five minutes no matter what you do, we finally pack Georgie into the car and head back to the apartment.

Once leftovers are put away and Georgie is wrangled into her pajamas, the three of us finally settle in for the night. Georgie curls up in the corner of the living room with a new toy, and Charlie and I collapse onto the couch together, legs tangling comfortably.

"You know," I say, leaning back against the cushions, willing myself to melt into them and let the remaining stress of the day fall away. "For all the chaos, tonight was pretty perfect."

Charlie hums in agreement, his shoulder brushing mine as he settles even closer against me, his head resting on my shoulder. "Your sister looked like she had a good time."

"Thanks to your brother," I say, nudging him playfully.

"Donnie's not subtle," Charlie replies, chuckling. "But he's a good guy. They'd be good for each other, I think."

"Georgie certainly thinks so," I say.

Charlie laughs, a warm, soft sound that settles something in my chest. "That kid's got a future as a rom-com writer... or a vicious dictator. Either one, really."

We sit in comfortable silence for a moment, watching Georgie play. The twinkle lights on the Christmas tree cast a soft glow over the room, and I can't help but feel overwhelmed by how right this all feels.

"Thanks for tonight," I say quietly.

Charlie looks at me, his expression softening. "For what?"

"For everything," I say, gesturing around. "For your family, for making us feel like we're part of it. For... this."

He smiles, leaning in to kiss my temple. "You don't have to thank me for that," he says. "You and Georgie are already family. This is just the start."

And in that moment, it feels like everything I've ever wanted is right here, within reach.

CHAPTER NINE

CHARLIE

DECEMBER 22ND

By Saturday afternoon, the brewery is decked out like a Hallmark Christmas movie exploded inside, even more so than before. Twinkling lights wrap around every exposed beam, garlands drape along every possible surface, and the tree in the corner is so loaded with ornaments Mac had to attach it to the ceiling with wire this morning to keep it from falling over.

Tonight's event is Spirit of Hops' annual *Pre-Game for the Holiday Party*, hosted on the Saturday before Christmas every year. It's the last hurrah before everyone before the full insanity of family dinners and obligations kicks in. For some, it's a chance to celebrate and unwind; for others, it's a chance to pre-game and brace themselves for the battle ahead. Zero judgement, we've all been there. I'm just glad we can be here and be part of people's traditions, whatever their reasons.

I'm stationed behind the bar, pulling pints and keeping an eye on the room as everyone else mingles and gets their party on. "Hey Em," I call over my shoulder toward Emily, who's behind the bar with me tonight. "Where are we on the cider kegs?"

Emily doesn't pause as she closes out a tab for one customer and opens one for another. "Switched them out twenty minutes ago. We're good."

"I knew I liked you."

"Convince Luka to finally hire us another bar back, and I'll consider it even," she shoots back, sliding a mug to a waiting customer.

"Only if they're not as much a pain in the ass as you," I reply, grabbing the next order. We settle into a rhythm, the hours passing more quickly than I notice.

Callum and Georgie arrive an hour after the event officially begins, just as the crowd is hitting its pre-dinner peak. Georgie's perched on his shoulders like the world's cutest tree topper as he ducks to get through the door and not bang her head on the casing. She's wearing her version of an ugly Christmas sweater with a sequined reindeer on the front. The little ball of sunshine waves excitedly as she sees me before wiggling enough to force her dad to set her down. Before her feet even hit the floor, she darts off toward the cookie decorating station set up near one of the garage doors, where Anya from the coffee shop helps kids wield frosting tubes like tiny, sugary swords.

Cal slides around the bar and settles next to me, looking effortlessly handsome in a red sweater and sporting a smile just for me, the kind of smile that makes his eyes crinkle in a way that should be illegal. "Busy night?"

"You mean a party specifically designed to get drunk before having to deal with your family for Christmas in a small town that treats free beer samples like a gold rush? No, not busy at all," I reply, leaning over to steal a quick kiss. It's hardly the most scandalous thing we've done in view of customers, but it still earns us a wolf whistle or two and a cat-call from Ollie, who's posted up on a barstool a few feet down from us.

"Stop distracting him, Cal," Ollie calls with a grin.

"No need to be a cockblock just cuz you're jealous I've only been gay for a few months, and I'm already better at it than you," I crack back. Stupid, juvenile, and most likely offensive to anyone who isn't my youngest brother? Most likely. But when has that ever stopped me from giving him hell?

"First of all—better at being gay??—yeah, not even gonna attempt to figure out what you mean with that one," Ollie says, rolling his eyes dramatically before turning to Callum. "Cal, it's not too late to run far, far away from this idiot. You know that, right? Blink twice if you need help. If the sounds coming from his room when he was in high school are anything to go by, there is no way it's *that* good to be worth putting up with his brand of bullshit."

Little brothers, I fucking swear...

"Ooh are we making fun of our brother's prowess or lack thereof? Count me in!" Sarah pipes up, slipping into the space beside Ollie at the bar. "You mean like how Cal used to call it his *no-no spot* weeeeelllll into high school, so there is absolutely no way the man has any level of dirty talk game?" she asks, sending both her and Ollie into peels of laughter.

"I really think we should be concerned our younger siblings have given this much thought into our sex life," Cal deadpans, shooting the pair of them an unimpressed look.

"Whose sex life are we making fun of now?" Donnie asks, stepping up behind Sarah with a grin. And no, none of us misses how he casually drapes an arm around her shoulders. I will absolutely be bringing that up again later. Thank you very much.

"Literally *any* of yours," Cal replies, doing his best 'big brother' face but falling short.

Really, they brought this upon themselves. "Great idea, Cal. I agree. So, we starting with Ollie and his revolving door of clients he absolutely doesn't fuck around with, or shall we start with you two and how Sarah hasn't been back to Cal's apartment since the family dinner… two days ago?" I ask, my tone casual but my expression daring them to say a fucking word.

"Aaaaand I'm out," Ollie says, spinning in his seat and dashing away through the crowd.

"What's that? Oh, I think I hear… mom… or Alfie calling for me… yeah…" Donnie hedges before snagging Sarah's hand and awkwardly trying to slink away.

Stumbling after him, Sarah shoots us a bewildered and slightly guilty look before turning and melting into the crowd on Donnie's heels.

"Rotten little shits, the lot of 'em," I laugh.

"Yeah, and whose bright idea was it to introduce my hellion of a sister to your demon-spawn brothers again?" Cal asks with a laugh, and all I can do is laugh right along with him until Emily calls my name and sucks me back into work for the next while as Callum joins the buzzing crowd to do his thing.

The night marches along in a blur of laughter, spilled drinks, and a heartwarming amount of familiar faces. Sloan, having closed the bar down early to help drive people here for the party, shows up with Lottie after a while, and they both immediately begin their favorite pastime—tormenting Kendric and Luka. Kendric simply watches the women's antics from his seat at a table in the corner with Sloan on his lap, while Luka looks like he is slowly and meticulously plotting Lottie's death. Mac even makes an appearance when he usually avoids bigger events like this when at all possible, albeit grumbling about the crowd size and noise, but clearly enjoying himself.

Even my brothers are behaving, well, mostly. Alfie and Ollie are charming their way through the room, while Donnie is deep in conversation with Sarah near the stage, where a local band is playing acoustic covers of Christmas classics. Can't say I could think of a better way for tonight to go.

Eventually, Kendic's voice calling my name cuts through the chatter, and I turn to see him pointing toward the stage. "It's time," he says as he steps up to the bar.

"Already?" I feign panic. "I thought I had at least ten more minutes to procrastinate."

"Move it," he says, arms crossed over his chest, with Sloan giggling next to him. Yes, giggling. I think someone might have had a bit too much to drink tonight. I will never get over seeing the 'take no shit' Sloan *giggle*. "And don't forget to smile."

With a dramatic sigh, I step away from the bar and make my way to the small stage. The chatter quiets as I tap the mic, and suddenly, all eyes are on me. Great. No pressure. It's not like the last time I was up here I confessed my undying love to the man of my dreams or anything. Not a hard act to follow, not at all. Why did I volunteer for this again?

"Hey! How's it goin' Rapids Bay?" I start, internally cringing at myself, but when it earns a cheer from the crowd, I decide to just go with it. "Thanks for coming out tonight and making our Christmas Pre-Game Party a success! Nights like these remind me why we do what we do here. Sure, the beer's great—especially the new toasted marshmallow stout —but it's the people that make this place special."

I pause, scanning the room. There's a familiar warmth in seeing so many people I know, from longtime regulars and family to first-timers. My gaze catches on Callum, standing near the bar with Georgie now perched on his hip. He's watching me, his expression soft and a little amused, and for a moment, I feel like we're the only two people here, and I can say this next part directly to him.

"This year, I've been reminded over and over again how lucky I am to have such incredible people in my life," I continue. "As a wise man said recently, this time of year is about family. Not just the ones you're born into, but the ones you build and find along the way. It's about finding joy in the chaos and making memories that'll keep you warm even long after the beer runs out."

There's a chuckle from the crowd, and I catch Georgie whispering something to Callum. His lips quirk into a smile, and it steadies me.

"So here's to all of you—our Rapids Bay family. To love, to laughter, and to the kind of nights that remind us why we keep showing up for each other. Cheers!"

"Cheers!" the crowd echoes, raising their glasses as applause ripples through the taproom. I step back, soaking in the moment for a beat as the band comes back on stage before my attention is pulled back to Callum. He's still looking at me, and his expression is enough to make my chest ache in the best way.

A few hours later, as the night finally winds down, I find myself standing beneath one of the many mistletoe clusters Emily and Lottie strategically placed around the taproom. Cal joins me, his expression caught somewhere between amused and exasperated.

"You planned this, didn't you?" he asks, nodding toward the little green bundle above my head.

"I'd never," I say, feigning innocence and failing miserably thanks to the grin I can't suppress. "It's a complete coincidence."

"Uh-huh," he responds, giving me a teasingly dubious look.

"Where's little miss thing?" I ask, my voice going warm and soft at his nearness.

"Nana Barbie declared it a girls' night, so both Georgie and Sarah are having a sleepover at your parents' place tonight. I think she kicked your dad out to one of your brother's places for the night, too," he laughs.

"So… we have a boys' night then?" I tease, unable to resist the joke.

Callum just cocks a judgemental brow at me in response. Fair enough, not my best work.

"My point stands; we've got the night off and should make the most of it," I counter.

He steps closer, close enough that the noise of the party fades into the background. "Well, since we're here…"

"Since we're here," I echo, my voice trailing off as he leans in.

The kiss is soft and sweet, and the rest of the world disappears for a moment. It's just us, standing in the glow of twinkling lights, surrounded by the warmth of a place that feels more like home every day.

When we finally pull back, Callum's smiling, his cheeks faintly pink. "Merry Christmas, Charlie."

"Merry Christmas, Callum," I reply, and for the first time all night, I'm perfectly still. "Take me home."

CHAPTER TEN

CALLUM

DECEMBER 22ND

The apartment is quiet except for the click of the door as it swings shut behind us. Charlie doesn't even bother to take his coat off. He turns, his grin sharp and full of mischief, and presses me back against the door.

"Subtle entrance," I manage, though my voice is already unsteady.

He shrugs, his hands sliding to my waist. "Why waste time being subtle? The party's over, and I've been waiting all night to get you alone."

I blink, trying to focus, but Charlie's already leaning in, his breath warm against my cheek. "You're bold tonight," I say, my words soft as his lips brush my jaw.

"I'm always bold," he murmurs, his voice low and teasing.

"True," I say, gripping his coat and tugging him closer.

Charlie has this ability to switch from playful to intense in a heartbeat, and right now, he's walking that line like a pro. His hands wander, exploring under my shirt as he kisses me again, this time slower, deeper.

Charlie's lips are soft and insistent, his touch sending shivers down my spine. I let out a small moan as he trails kisses down my neck, his hands sliding under my shirt to explore every inch of skin. I cling to him, feeling dizzy with desire as he presses me against the door. His mouth moves back up to mine, and I can taste the faint tang of alcohol on his breath.

"Is this okay?" he asks between kisses.

I nod eagerly, unable to form words as he continues his assault on my senses. His hands travel lower, teasing at the waistband of my jeans before slipping inside. I gasp at his touch, the sensation sending a jolt of electricity through me. Charlie smirks against my lips, clearly pleased with himself for getting this reaction out of me.

My mind is clouded with desire, and I lose myself in the moment, allowing Charlie to lead us toward the couch, where we collapse in a tangle of limbs.

He pulls away for a moment to catch his breath and looks at me with an intensity that makes my heart race. "You're so gorgeous," he whispers before diving back in for another passionate kiss.

Our bodies move together in perfect harmony, melting into each other as we explore every plane and angle. Each touch sends electric shocks of pleasure through me, and I never want this moment to end. The heat between us intensifies, causing my breath to hitch as he pulls away slightly to meet my gaze. His eyes are deep and focused, taking in every detail of our passionate connection.

"Bedroom," I whisper, the word more a suggestion than a demand.

His grin turns wolfish. "Bossy."

"You like it," I shoot back, but it's half-hearted because

Charlie's already tugging me off the couch and guiding me down the hall, his hands never leaving me.

We don't make it to the bed right away. Halfway there, he pushes me against the wall, capturing my mouth again, pinning between his rocking hips and the plaster. I lose myself in his taste, the way his laugh vibrates against my lips when I groan in frustration.

"You're impossible," I say, my voice breaking between kisses.

"And you love it."

I don't argue.

By the time we finally stumble into my bedroom, the tension between us is thick, electric. Charlie shrugs out of his shirt, tossing it to the floor with dramatic flair.

"I hope you don't mind," he says, stepping toward me, his grin softening. "I plan to stay for a while."

"As if I'd let you leave," I say, reaching for him.

His expression shifts, the humor fading just slightly as something deeper settles in. "Callum," he says quietly, his hands resting on my shoulders.

"Yeah?"

"You know I'm all in, right?" His tone is steady, but there's a vulnerability beneath it. "With you, with Georgie... this isn't just a... this is it for me."

My chest tightens, not with fear or uncertainty, but with the sheer force of how much I feel for him. I nod, cupping his face in my hands. "I know. And it's the same for me. For both of us."

His lips curve into a soft smile that steals my breath more than anything else. "Good. Just making sure."

The heat between us doesn't take long to reignite, though it's slower, more deliberate this time. Every touch, every kiss, feels like a promise, a declaration that what we have is real, solid, unshakable. We undress each other with a sense of reverence, taking our time to explore every inch of each other's bodies. Our movements are slow and intentional, fueled by our intense connection.

Charlie's fingers trail down my chest, his touch feather-light yet electrifying. He leans in, pressing soft kisses along my collarbone as his hands explore lower. I shiver, over-whelmed by the sensations he's stirring within me.

"Charlie," I breathe, my voice thick with desire.

He looks up, his eyes dark and intense. Without a word, he guides me onto the bed, his body covering mine. The weight of him is comforting, grounding. His skin is warm against mine as we move together, finding a rhythm that feels as natural as breathing.

I run my hands down his back, feeling the muscles shift beneath my fingers. Charlie's lips find that sensitive spot just below my ear, and I arch into him, a low moan escaping me. He chuckles softly; the sound vibrating against my skin.

"Sensitive there, are we?"

"You know I am," I murmur, tangling my fingers in his hair.

Charlie hums contentedly, nuzzling against my neck as his hands roam lower. His touch ignites sparks beneath my skin, each caress stoking the fire building between us. I let my own hands wander, tracing the planes of his back, feeling goosebumps rise in their wake.

Our lips meet again in a deep, languid kiss. Charlie takes his time, alternating between gentle nibbles and searing intensity. His tongue sweeps against mine, tasting of whiskey and desire. I'm intoxicated by him, drunk on the feeling of skin on skin and how he makes my pulse race.

As our kisses grow more heated, Charlie shifts his weight, aligning our bodies. The friction sends shockwaves of plea-sure through me. I gasp, breaking the kiss to throw my head back against the pillows.

"Fuck, so good," I gasp, and the bastard only chuckles.

As Charlie presses against me, I'm lost in a haze of sensation. His lips trace a fiery path down my neck, each kiss igniting sparks beneath my skin. I arch into him, craving more contact, more friction. My fingers dig into his shoulders as he works his way lower, exploring every dip and plane of my pecs, nuzzling into the dusting of hair there and taking a deep, drugging inhale, letting it out on a quiet growl.

Charlie takes his time, lavishing attention on my chest, my stomach, and the sensitive skin of my inner thighs. His touch is reverent, almost worshipful. When he finally takes me in his mouth, I cry out, overwhelmed by the wet heat enveloping me, the teasing drag of his fingertips tracing up my inner thigh and over my sac, already drawn up tight against my body. My hips buck involuntarily, but Charlie's strong hands hold me steady.

He works me with expert precision, alternating between quick, teasing swirls around the head, mind-altering flicks of the tip of his tongue against my frenulum, and just when I think I will lose my damn mind and my load entirely too soon, the wicked man takes me all the way down, swallowing around me when my crown hits the back of his throat.

"Fucking HELL, Charlie! Fuck, so good," I cry out, gripping him tight, trying everything I can to hold on and fend off my release. I writhe beneath Charlie's ministrations, lost in a haze of pleasure. His tongue swirls and teases, bringing me to the edge before easing back. My fingers tangle in his hair as I struggle to maintain some semblance of control.

"Charlie," I gasp, tugging gently. "I need you. Please."

He releases me with a soft pop, crawling back up my body. His eyes are dark, pupils blown wide with desire. "What do you need, love?" he murmurs, nuzzling against my neck.

"You. Inside me. Now," I manage, words failing me as he grinds his hips against mine.

Charlie's hands tremble slightly as he opens the bottle of lube from the nightstand, his eyes never leaving mine. I spread my legs wider in invitation, breath catching as he traces feather-light circles around my entrance.

"Relax for me, love," he murmurs, pressing a gentle kiss behind my ear.

I take a deep breath, willing my body to loosen as Charlie slowly pushes a finger inside. The initial stretch burns slightly, but Charlie is patient, working me open with careful, deliberate movements. Pleasure has overtaken any discomfort by the time he adds a second finger.

Charlie crooks his fingers just so, and I arch off the bed with a gasp. "There," I pant, grinding down against his hand. "Right there."

He grins, repeating the motion as he works a third finger inside me.

Charlie's fingers work their magic, stretching and teasing until I'm a quivering mess beneath him. My skin feels electric, every nerve ending alight with pleasure. When he finally withdraws his fingers, I whimper at the loss.

"Shh, I've got you," he soothes, positioning himself between my legs.

The blunt pressure of him against my entrance makes me gasp. Charlie pauses, his eyes searching mine. "You okay?"

I nod, wrapping my legs around his waist to pull him closer. "Don't you dare fucking stop, Charlie. I need you."

He pushes forward slowly, giving me time to adjust to the stretch. The burn is exquisite, pleasure and pain mingling as he fills me completely. When he's fully seated, we both pause, panting. Charlie's forehead rests against mine, our breaths mingling. His arms tremble slightly.

Charlie's arms tremble as he holds himself above me, his eyes locked on mine. The intensity of his gaze makes my breath catch. Slowly, he begins to move, pulling out almost entirely before pushing back in with agonizing slowness. The drag of him inside me sends sparks of pleasure radiating through my body. I grip his shoulders, my fingers digging into taut muscle as he sets a steady rhythm. Each thrust is measured, deliberate, hitting that spot inside me that makes me see stars.

"God, Callum," Charlie groans, his voice rough with desire. "You feel amazing."

I can only moan in response, lost in the sensations coursing through me. Charlie's skin is slick with sweat, sliding against mine as we move together. The room fills with the sounds of our ragged breathing and the creak of the bed beneath us. Charlie shifts his angle slightly, and I swear I see stars as he pegs my prostate with laser precision. The heat building at the base of my spine ramps up with each thrust, the friction of him inside me bringing me closer and closer to the edge. I wrap my legs around him, pulling him deeper.

"Charlie," I gasp. "Oh, fuck."

He drops his head to the crook of my neck, his breath hot on my skin. He kisses and sucks at the tender flesh, leaving a trail of bruises in his wake. I arch into him, desperate for more. His thrusts grow more erratic, his rhythm faltering as we both near our release. I cling to him, lost in a haze of pleasure.

"I'm so close," I pant.

"Me too," Charlie says, his voice ragged. "Fuck, Cal."

He presses a hand between us, his fingers finding my aching cock, finally giving it the attention it needs. He strokes me in time with his thrusts, and I feel myself teetering on the edge. He's gotten me to come hands-free before, but no way in hell do I have the patience for the buildup that is required tonight.

"Charlie," I gasp, the warning clear in my tone.

"Come for me, Callum," he whispers, his lips brushing against my ear.

With a strangled cry, I fall over the edge, my climax crashing through me like a wave. My entire body trembles as the pleasure rolls through me, every nerve ending alight with ecstasy as my release fills his fist.

Charlie's hips stutter, and with a final, deep thrust, he finds his release. He moans my name as he spills inside me, his cock throbbing against my tightening walls. We cling to each other, riding out the aftershocks of our pleasure, until at last, Charlie collapses beside me, panting for breath. I lie beside him, staring up at the ceiling, feeling utterly spent.

"Holy shit," Charlie gasps, his chest heaving.

"Yeah," I agree, the word coming out as more of a wheeze than a word.

"I think I died and went to heaven," Charlie says, a lazy smile spreading across his face.

I chuckle, turning my head to look at him. His blonde hair is mussed, his cheeks flushed, and his blue eyes bright. He looks thoroughly satisfied, and I feel a spark of pride knowing I'm the reason for it.

Charlie's expression softens, and he leans over to kiss me. His lips are warm and soft, and the taste of him is like coming home. I could spend hours kissing him like this and never grow tired of it. But all too soon, he pulls away, and a shiver runs through me as his absence leaves me cold.

"We should get cleaned up," he says.

"Yeah," I agree, though I'd much rather stay right where I am, tangled up in him.

Reluctantly, we pull ourselves out of bed, and Charlie leads me to the bathroom.

After a quick shower—and another round of blowjobs under the warm spray—we settle into bed and quickly tangle under the covers once again. The room is quiet except for the soft rustle of sheets and our breathing. Charlie rests his head on my chest, his fingers tracing lazy patterns along my side and through the curls of chest hair.

"You know," he says after a moment, his voice low, "I've been thinking."

"Uh-oh," I tease, earning a half-hearted swat to my stomach.

"Shut up," he says, but I can feel his smile against my skin. "I'm serious. I've been thinking about what's next for us."

I shift, glancing down at him. "Oh yeah? And what's the verdict?"

Charlie takes a deep breath, but there's no hesitation in his expression. "I want to be clear: I'm all in. With you, with Georgie, with this whole thing we've built. I'm not sitting here wondering if it's right or if it's going to work—I already know it is."

My chest tightens, not with fear but with something far warmer. "I know it, too," I say. "I've known it for a while now."

His smile turns soft, his hand finding mine. "Good. Because I'm not interested in playing it safe or slow. I'm ready for what's next—whatever that looks like for us."

I squeeze his hand, my words steady. "I'm ready, too. For me, it's you and Georgie. That's it. You're already family, Charlie."

His eyes glint with something that looks suspiciously like unshed tears, though he'd never admit it. "So... what does that mean? Are we talking moving in? Bigger plans?"

A laugh escapes me, light and relieved. "All of it. I mean, I can't guarantee Georgie won't take over your life with glitter and stuffed animals, but if you're up for it..."

Charlie leans in, his voice a soft murmur. "Up for it? Callum, I've been waiting for you to say that since the day Georgie first handed me a picture she drew of all three of us. Stick figures, sure, but the message was clear."

I laugh; the image of that drawing is vivid in my mind. "She's subtle like that."

"Wonder where she gets that from," he teases, and before I can respond, his lips are on mine.

The kiss deepens, the conversation falling away as we give in to the pull that's always been there. Charlie's hands find their way to my waist, tugging me closer as my fingers curl around his strong biceps again. When we finally break apart, both of us breathless, he presses his forehead to mine.

"So," he whispers, his voice laced with a mix of humor and something deeper, "this is what 'next steps' feels like, huh?"

I grin, tugging him closer. "You've got no idea."

CHAPTER ELEVEN

CHARLIE

DECEMBER 25TH

I wake up to the sound of tiny feet thundering down the hall and a high-pitched squeal that's too enthusiastic for this hour. Before I can fully process what's happening, the bedroom door slams open, and Georgie appears, curls sticking up in every direction, her little "King Kon" stuffie clutched under one arm.

"Santa came!" she shrieks, diving onto the bed like a rocket. She lands squarely between Callum and me, her knee driving into my ribs, pulling a pained groan from me.

"Oof—good morning to you, too," I manage, groaning as I try to sit up.

The bed jolts again, and my groggy mind catches up as Georgie scrambles over me like a squirrel on a caffeine high. Callum stirs beside me, muttering something unintelligible before turning his head toward the commotion.

"Georgie," he groans, voice raspy from sleep, "it's too early for this."

"It's never too early for Christmas!" she exclaims, her tiny hands patting his face enthusiastically. "Come on, Dad! Charles! Let's see what Santa brought!"

I blink blearily at her and then at Callum, who's trying to untangle himself from the blankets while fending off whirl-wind Georgie, while somehow making zero progress on either front.

"I take it back," I mumble. "She's not a squirrel; she's a tornado."

Georgie giggles, turning her energy on me. "Come on, Charles!" she tugs on my arm. "You have to get up, too! This is a family thing!"

Callum grunts and flips onto his back, glaring at her with one eye open. "Georgie, let Charlie live. He's not used to our brand of morning chaos this early."

She crosses her arms, her tiny frame vibrating with impatience. "He's part of the family now. He can handle it."

That stops both of us in our tracks. I glance over at him, and his soft, sleepy smile nearly undoes me.

"Out of the mouths of babe," he murmurs, and I can feel the warmth of his words sink into my chest.

"Alright, alright," I say, sitting up and ruffling Georgie's hair. "Let's go see what Santa brought. But I'm going to need coffee first."

"Fine," she says, clearly appeased for now. "But hurry!" She wriggles away with a delighted squeal, sliding off the bed and bouncing on her toes.

Callum manages to sit up fully, running a hand through his sleep-mussed hair and shooting me a tired but fond smile.

"You regret staying over yet?" he asks, his tone teasing, but his eyes warm.

"Not even a little," I reply, stretching. "Wouldn't miss this for the world." I lean over and kiss his shoulder, enjoying the way he smiles, soft and genuine, at the contact.

"Okay, okay, are we going, or are you two just gonna sit there and stare at each other all morning?" Georgie demands, hands on her hips.

Callum snorts and swings his legs over the side of the bed. "Alright, tornado. Let's go see what Santa brought."

The living room looks like something out of a Christmas card. The tree is glowing with soft white lights, and beneath it is a pile of presents that practically takes up the entire corner.

Georgie freezes for a second, her eyes wide as she takes it all in. "Whoa," she breathes, inching closer like she's afraid it might disappear if she moves too fast.

I glance at Callum, and his face is pure dad-pride. It's adorable.

"Can I—" Georgie starts, looking at us with a barely restrained excitement.

"Breakfast first," Callum says, cutting her off before she can finish.

She groans, flopping dramatically onto the couch. "But I'm gonna diiiie of waiting!"

"You'll live," Callum replies, smirking as he heads toward the kitchen. "Come on, Charlie. Help me keep her alive while I make coffee."

"I'll try, but no promises," I say, following him.

"But—"

"No buts," I interject, grabbing a plate of prepped cinnamon rolls from the fridge. "Good things come to those who wait."

Georgie narrows her eyes at me in mock betrayal before scampering back to the living room.

Callum shakes his head, chuckling. "You're good with her."

"She makes it easy," I say, nudging him with my elbow.

His smile deepens, and I can see something unspoken flicker in his expression, something warm and full of meaning.

By the time the coffee is brewed, and the cinnamon rolls are golden, we join Georgie in the living room. She's arranged all the presents into piles, each labeled by owner.

"Okay!" she announces, bouncing on the balls of her feet. "We have to open them together. That's the rule."

"What rule?" Callum asks, eyebrow raised.

"Our family rule!" she says, as if it's the most obvious thing in the world.

My chest tightens at her words, a rush of emotion leaving me momentarily speechless.

"Well," Callum says, sitting down on the couch and patting the spot next to him. "Can't argue with family rules."

"Okay, Georgie," Callum says with a grin. "Go for it."

She tears into the first package like a tornado, wrapping paper flying everywhere as she pulls out a dollhouse she's been begging for since September.

"Santa brought it! He really brought it!" she screams, hugging the box like it's the love of her life.

I glance at Callum, who's watching her with this look on his face that makes me want to kiss him senseless.

"This is the good stuff, huh?" I murmur, nudging his shoulder.

He looks over at me, his smile softening. "Yeah, it is."

The next hour is a blur of ripped wrapping paper, delighted squeals, and Callum and me exchanging amused glances as Georgie works her way through her haul.

Finally, when the floor is littered with colorful paper and ribbons, Georgie declares, "Now it's your turn!"

She hands Callum a small box with her name scrawled on the tag in shaky six-year-old handwriting.

"I wrapped it myself," she says proudly as he carefully peels back the paper. Inside is a mug with the words *Best Dad Ever* painted in Georgie's unmistakable handwriting.

Callum blinks, his mouth opening slightly like he wants to say something but can't quite find the words.

"Do you like it?" Georgie asks, bouncing on her heels.

"Georgie," he says softly, his voice thick. "I love it. Thank you."

Her smile could light up the whole block.

Callum's eyes go glassy as he holds it up. "Georgie, this is perfect. Thank you."

"You're welcome!" she says, beaming.

She hands me a similar box, and when I open it, I find another mug that says *Best Double-Daddy Ever.*

My throat tightens, and I glance at Callum, who looks just as stunned as I feel.

"Georgie," I say, looking up at her, then at Callum. "This is… this is perfect."

"You're part of the family now, right?" she says, as if it's the most obvious thing in the world.

Callum's eyes meet mine, and there's something steady and certain that makes my chest feel tight.

"Now you can match!" she says, beaming.

"Matching mugs," Callum says. "It's official. We're a team."

Georgie nods. "A family team."

Callum's gaze shifts to me, and the world narrows to just the three of us for a moment.

"Yeah," he says quietly. "We are."

The rest of the morning is a blur of wrapping paper, laughter, and more cinnamon rolls than I should probably admit to eating.

When the last gift is opened, and the living room looks like a hurricane of ribbons and boxes, Georgie insists on setting up her new dollhouse immediately.

"Priorities," Callum says, winking at me as he helps her piece it together.

I watch them, my heart full as I take in the way Callum patiently guides her tiny hands and the way she lights up every time he praises her.

By the time evening rolls around, Georgie is fast asleep on the couch, her new doll clutched tightly in her arms. Callum and I sit side by side on the floor, leaning against the couch as we watch the lights on the tree twinkle.

"She's amazing," I say quietly, breaking the comfortable silence.

"She is," Callum agrees, his voice soft.

I glance at him, my heart full as I take in the way the light from the tree reflects in his eyes.

"Thank you," I say, my voice just as soft. "For letting me be a part of this. Of her life."

Callum turns to me, his gaze steady and warm. "Charlie, you're not just part of her life. You're part of ours. You are ours."

For a moment, all I can do is look at him, my heart so full it feels like it might burst.

"Merry Christmas," I say finally, leaning in to kiss him.

"Merry Christmas," he whispers back, his lips warm and sure against mine.

And in that moment, I know without a doubt—this is home. This is forever.

CHAPTER TWELVE

CALLUM

DECEMBER 31ST

The brewery hums with energy as the final hours of the year tick away. Laughter, clinking glasses, and the thrum of music fill the space, blending into one big, joyful celebration. I'm leaning against the end of the bar, taking a rare breather while Charlie works the crowd. His laugh cuts through the noise, bright and infectious, as he hands off another round of drinks to one of the regulars.

Even now, I can't help but watch him. He moves so effortlessly between customers, throwing out a joke here, a compliment there; he's completely in his element, and damn if it doesn't make my chest tighten a little.

"Daddy!"

Georgie's voice pulls me out of my thoughts just as she darts through a group of adults, her sparkly headband slightly askew and her cheeks flushed from running around.

"Hey, munchkin." I bend to catch her, laughing as she throws her arms around my neck.

"Nana Barbie gave me two cookies," she announces, her tone both triumphant and slightly conspiratorial.

"Two?" I raise an eyebrow, glancing toward the corner where Charlie's mom is chatting with a group of regulars and Betha. She winks at me over the rim of her glass. "She's spoiling you."

Georgie shrugs, completely unbothered. "She said it's because I'm the cutest one here."

"Hard to argue with that," I admit, brushing a strand of hair from her face. "Having fun?"

She nods vigorously. "Yep! But do you know what time it is?"

I glance at the clock above the bar. "It's almost ten."

Her eyes light up. "That means only two more hours until fireworks! Can I stay up? Pleeeease?"

I laugh. "We'll see if you can make it that long. No promises."

Her pout lasts all of two seconds before she spots Charlie heading our way.

"Charlie!" she squeals, squirming out of my arms to run to him.

He crouches to meet her halfway, lifting her into a hug as if she weighs nothing. "Hey, superstar. Did you already charm Nana Barbie out of more cookies?"

"She gave me two!" Georgie declares proudly, holding up two fingers for emphasis.

"Two cookies? Wow, you're living the dream." He sets her down gently, ruffling her hair before turning to me. "How's it going over here?"

"Just trying to keep up," I say, tipping my glass toward him. "You look like you're in full host mode."

He smirks. "It's my superpower. Speaking of which, you mind stepping outside with me for a second?"

I raise an eyebrow, curious, but nod. "Sure. Georgie, stay with Nana Barbie, okay? I'll be right back."

She barely acknowledges me, too busy showing off her sparkly headband to one of Charlie's brothers.

"You look like you could use a break," he says as Georgie scurries off, his tone light, but his eyes tracking me in that way that makes my heart do a little stutter step.

"Breaks are for people who don't have a kid running around trying to unionize the food truck crew," I quip, but I can feel myself soften under his gaze.

Charlie leans closer, his voice dropping just enough to send a little shiver down my spine. "I mean it. Come with me. Just for a minute."

I raise an eyebrow. "You're not about to steal me away for some grand romantic gesture, are you?"

"Maybe," he says with a smirk. "Just humor me, Callum."

I follow him around the bar, weaving past clumps of revelers and dodging the occasional flying party hat. He leads me toward the back, where the sound of the crowd fades to a hum, and the only light comes from the muted glow of the overhead fixtures and the faint sparkle of the brewery's decorations.

"What are we doing back here?" I ask, trying to keep my voice casual despite the sudden, inexplicable flutter of nerves in my chest.

"Dancing," he says, setting the tray down on a nearby counter and turning to face me.

I blink. "Dancing?"

"Yeah, you know, that thing where two people move in vaguely coordinated patterns and pretend they're not completely ridiculous?"

I snort, but he doesn't give me a chance to respond before he steps closer, sliding one hand into mine and resting the other lightly on my waist.

"Charlie—"

"Shh," he murmurs, his grin softening into something quieter, something deeper. "Just go with it."

There's no music back here, but the faint echo of whatever upbeat track is playing in the main room filters through the walls enough to give us a rhythm to follow. I let him lead; our movements slow and a little awkward but somehow perfect, anyway.

"This is ridiculous," I mutter, even as I feel my shoulders relax and a grin tug at the corner of my mouth.

"Maybe," he says, his eyes locking on mine. "But it's also kind of perfect, isn't it?"

I don't have a response to that, at least not one that wouldn't sound completely sappy, so I just nod.

We move in lazy circles, the world outside shrinking to just the two of us. And for a moment, I let myself get lost in it —in the warmth of his hand on mine, the way his eyes crinkle when he smiles, the steady thrum of his presence grounding me in a way I didn't know I needed.

I'm not sure how long we go on like that, but after a while, Charlie pulls back and looks at me. There's a flicker of something in his expression—nervous, maybe? Seeing him like this is rare, and it immediately grabs my attention.

"Charlie?" I prompt, my tone softening.

"Callum, do you know my favorite thing about this year?"

I tilt my head, smirking. "Let me guess—when I finally gave in and agreed to go out with you?"

He laughs, the sound low and warm. "That's a close second. But no, my favorite thing about this year is that it gave me you and Georgie. Us."

He steps closer, cupping my face with both hands, his thumb brushing along my jaw.

"We talked the other night," he says, his voice steady but filled with emotion. "And we agreed we're in this for the long haul. No hesitation. No doubts. And I've been thinking about what that looks like, what comes next for us."

I swallow hard, my heart racing in anticipation.

"I want us to live together," he says simply, his eyes locked on mine. "You, me, Georgie. I want to wake up every day with you next to me, with her running into our room to wake us up because she's too excited to wait for pancakes. I want Georgie to know that I'm always there for her. I want us to be a family, Callum. Officially. Move in with me. Both of you."

I stare at him for a moment, my heart swelling so fast it feels like it might burst.

"You're serious," I say, though it's not a question.

"Completely," he says, his grip on my hands tightening slightly. "I know it's not a small thing, and I know this is fast, but I've never been more sure about anything in my life. You and Georgie—you're it for me."

I can't help the laugh that escapes me, equal parts relief and joy. "Charlie Larson, you're unbelievable."

"Unbelievable in a good way?" he asks, grinning.

"The best way," I say.

The relief and joy that flood his face are enough to make my knees go weak, and before I can say anything else, he's pulling me into a kiss.

It's soft and sweet at first, but then his hand slides up to cup my jaw, and suddenly it's anything but. The world tilts, and I lose myself in the feel of him, in the way he pours everything he can't put into words into this moment.

When we finally pull back, both of us breathless, he rests his forehead against mine, a smile tugging at his lips.

"Best New Year's ever," he murmurs.

We return to the party just in time for the final count-down, Georgie bouncing on her toes as she waits for us by the bar.

"There you are!" she exclaims, grabbing both our hands and pulling us toward the center of the room.

The crowd counts down together, voices loud and full of excitement.

"Three! Two! One! Happy New Year!"

Cheers erupt, glasses clink, and Georgie throws her arms around both of us, her laughter echoing through the room.

"Best New Year's ever!" she declares, her face lit up with pure joy.

Charlie meets my gaze over her head, his smile soft and full of love.

"Yeah," I say, my voice quiet but sure. "It really is."

Fireworks burst outside, painting the night sky in brilliant colors, but all I can focus on is the two of them—my daughter, my partner, my family.

This is everything I've ever wanted. And it's just the beginning.

ACKNOWLEDGMENTS

First off, I have to thank C&C, my brewery boys for not only giving me the inspiration for the entire Spirit of Hops series, but also for being on the covers and being such amazing sports about their random little brush with minor fame. You two are my favorites.

Also thank you to Rey for loving Georgie even more than I do and convincing me this little family needed another little slice of life Hallmark Movie moment.

Last but certainly not least, to my wonderful hubster. Thank you for putting up with my scatterbrained ridiculousness when I get lost in a story, your support and understanding when it comes to giving me the space and ability to explore my passion, and for not citing the mountain of unwashed dishes in any future letters of complaint or divorce filings ☺ (Oh I'm only joking.. you're stuck with me forever mwhahahah)

STALK J.E. JOYCE

Facebook:
https://www.facebook.com/j.e.joyce.author

Goodreads:
https://www.goodreads.com/author/show/24510228.
J_E_Joyce

Bookbub:
https://www.bookbub.com/authors/j-e-joyce

Instagram:
https://www.instagram.com/author.j.e.joyce/

ABOUT THE AUTHOR

J.E. Joyce lives in the frozen hellscape *cough* sorry, the lovely snow-covered dreamscape that is Minnesota. She is an unrepentant coffee addict, lifelong Broadway fanatic and theater geek, and thinks Deadpool absolutely counts as a chick flick. When she isn't melting pages with the steamy dreamy book boyfriends in her head, she's annoying the ever-loving heck outta her hubster and two mini monsters.